"Trent," Tara murmured.

His name on her lips was like a seductive whisper. He felt frozen in time. He stared at her, noticing how her hair moved in the light breeze. She was staring back. She looked shocked, as if she couldn't believe what she was seeing. He didn't blame her; he'd arrived on her doorstep, a memory of her past, without warning.

She looked at him as if seeing him for the first time. "Is it really you?"

"It is," he said, and only wanted to hug her, to touch her. Even to tell her how sorry he was to have left her the way he had all those years ago. He'd apologized for none of that. Even when her father had died, he'd not contacted her. Now he stood and waited for her to decide on what the next move would be. And he wondered if the past could be redone, if he would have done any better.

MARSHAL ON A MISSION

RYSHIA KENNIE

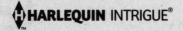

This book is dedicated to you, the reader. Enjoy!

ISBN-13: 978-1-335-60467-5

Marshal on a Mission

Copyright © 2019 by Patricia Detta

Recycling programs
for this product may
not exist in your area.

This edition published by arrangement with Harlequin Books S.A.

For questions and comments about the quality of this book, please contact us at CustomerService@Harlequin.com.

® and TM are trademarks of Harlequin Enterprises Limited or its corporate affiliates. Trademarks indicated with ® are registered in the United States Patent and Trademark Office, the Canadian Intellectual Property Office and in other countries.

Printed in U.S.A.

Ryshia Kennie has received a writing award from the City of Regina, Saskatchewan, and was also a semifinalist for the Kindle Book Awards. She finds that there's never a lack of places to set an edge-of-the-seat suspense, as prairie winters find her dreaming of warmer places for heart-stopping stories. They are places where deadly villains threaten intrepid heroes and heroines who battle for their right to live, or even to love. For more, visit ryshiakennie.com.

Books by Ryshia Kennie

Harlequin Intrigue

American Armor

Wanted by the Marshal
Marshal on a Mission

Desert Justice

Sheik's Rule
Sheik's Rescue
Son of the Sheik
Sheik Defense

Suspect Witness

Visit the Author Profile page at Harlequin.com.

CAST OF CHARACTERS

Trent Nielsen—Marshal assigned to the case. He has a past that includes the woman he's assigned to protect. But he's the one who knows her the best. What he doesn't know is the danger she faces when she leaves the United States behind.

Tara Munroe—Witness to a bank robbery who has a past of her own. She knows what can happen to the witness of a crime, but she's not prepared for what she needs to do to prevent it.

Carlos Martinez—A retired police officer who is determined to help—or is he? Some of his actions may be questionable.

Francesca Martinez—Silently supports her husband even when he may be in the wrong.

Enrique Gonzales—Second-in-command of the Mexican Federal Police, he has access to information and resources that could be used on either side of the law.

Jackson Vidal—The FBI agent who heads this case is determined to close it successfully and bring the witness home, no matter what needs to be done.

Lucas Cruz—He's desperate, for he has everything to lose.

Chapter One

The icy chill of déjà vu crept down her spine as if it had all happened only yesterday, and as if tragedy were about to happen again. Tara Munroe pushed the uneasy feeling away.

"It was a long time ago," she assured herself. But today, for some reason, it felt like yesterday that her father had been murdered. She knew that some things you never recovered from. Painful experience had taught her that. Some things left a mark no matter how long ago they had happened. She took a breath, trying to go back to enjoying the beautiful spring day. But something seemed to hang over her like a shadow.

"Forget it," she said to herself. She was being ridiculous, dreaming up trouble where there was none. Though it was the anniversary of that dreadful day. She took a deep breath. It wasn't an anniversary to remember. Instead she had to think of it as what it was, a beautiful day, midmorning, midspring.

It was already comfortably warm, touched with the lazy humidity left by last night's gentle rain. The sweet scent of petunias wafted from a planter on the city sidewalk. The flowers were early, grown in the local city greenhouse and just recently planted here. In the midst of downtown Pueblo, Colorado, the natural beauty of the flowers stood out against the brick and stone. The historic buildings that populated the downtown provided a touch of Old World to the city's core. But it was the sweet, earthy scent of the flowers that made her fingers itch to pick up a paintbrush and transfer the vibrant colors onto canvas or cardstock for greeting cards or...

But she had other things on her mind today, less artsy things—like getting some cash to pay her rent.

The last thought dropped as she was shoved, the arm of a man ramming into her shoulder and throwing her off balance. She had to catch herself from falling as she fought for balance, the clasp on her purse releasing. The hand-painted bag flew open, spilling some of its contents on the sidewalk.

"Hey!" she said as she bent down to pick up her things.

The man was already ahead of her. But he glanced back. His eyes briefly met hers, and in that moment, she noticed dark hair that was thick, short and wild, and the tawny color of his skin that accentuated a thick scar. The scar ran crookedly across the top half of his cheek. There was anger in his dark brown eyes and a wildness that made her heart race in fear.

A few feet away, he squatted down to pick up a rectangle of off-white paper with an elastic at one end. It looked like a medical mask. But that seemed a weird thing to carry around, she thought as she watched him shove it in his pocket and walk away without giving her a second look.

Jerk.

His lack of manners had her fuming. She kept watching him. She wasn't sure why, except that something about him felt a bit off. She watched as he crossed the street. Then he turned toward a familiar building, the same place she was headed: Pueblo First National Bank.

"Great," she muttered. Sitting on her haunches, she picked up the remainder of her things from the sidewalk and put them back into her purse.

A few minutes later, she opened the door to the bank and was met by a rush of air-conditioned chill that made her feel like winter had returned. She shivered and stopped. The silence was heavy, different from the usual buzz of business. And when she looked toward the tellers, she forgot to breathe.

The tellers seemed frozen in place as two men stood with handguns aimed at them. A third man was in her peripheral vision, but it was a movement to her left, a fourth man, that got her attention. She recognized that lanky build, the faded jeans and the gray T-shirt. He turned, and their eyes met. Like the others, he wore a mask—the surgical mask she'd seen earlier, the one he'd dropped.

Shock raced through her. She knew those eyes. She'd seen that face. It seemed like forever as she stared into hard, wild eyes she'd never forget, and saw again the edge of that vicious scar…and something else. He was armed, and he was aiming that gun at her.

She turned, took two steps back to the door, ducked and pushed the door open just as she heard a sound that she'd heard so many times before. She knew that sound. Her heart seemed to stop and then speed up into a wild hammering that screamed at her to get out. It was the sound she'd heard so often as a child during hunting season on the small hobby ranch where she'd grown up. A gunshot.

Glass shattered in front of her. Her heart was pumping loud enough that she was sure everyone could hear it. She bolted through the lobby door, grabbed the outside door and yanked it open. She was desperate to escape. Another bang and more glass rained down around her. And then she burst onto the street.

She ran as hard and as fast as she could. She was in a state of panic for the first block as she almost collided with a woman going the opposite direction.

"Go back! Bank robbery," she warned and repeated that warning at everyone she passed. Most looked at her oddly.

In the distance, sirens wailed. She waved wildly when the first of the sheriff's vehicles arrived. The vehicles flew past her followed by the second, a third after that.

"Armed robbery," she said in a panicked rush to the first deputy to pull over. "Four of them. They shot, they…" She was so freaked out she couldn't remember exactly what had happened. "I was there.

I saw one of them on the street before the robbery."
What else had she seen? Her hands shook so hard that
she could barely stand, never mind think of details.

"It's all right," the deputy said and opened the
back door of his vehicle.

She stood there frozen as if the invitation had
never been issued, as if the last minutes had never
happened.

"Get in, miss," the deputy said, his silver hair
glinting in the sunlight. "You're safe now."

She looked at him and reality returned. She saw
his badge, his uniform as he repeated his instruction. She crawled into the back seat, feeling only
slightly safer.

"We've got a witness," she heard the deputy report
seconds later.

A block away, she could see the convoy of flashing lights outside the bank. "Was anyone hurt?"

"No," he said. "I'll take your statement at the office."

She shook her head as panic ran through her. "I
can't remember his face or what happened. I'm sorry.
I—" Her voice broke off. "I bumped into him earlier
and I saw his face unmasked."

"Unmasked?" the deputy repeated.

"Yes." She nodded. "But now it's just too much.
Would it be all right to do this tomorrow? Everything is a blur."

"No. We'd like to interview you when it's fresh."

But an hour later in the sheriff's office, the deputy
looked at her in frustration. She was blanking out

on every question. She couldn't help it. Only once before had she ever been this shaken and not even then. She'd been too young.

"I'm sorry, I'm just..." She paused, not sure what she was. "Maybe tomorrow."

"Traumatized," he finished for her. "The morning will have to do." He looked at his watch. "Let's say eight o'clock. I'll bring a sketch artist to your house and we'll do a complete interview then."

After that, he drove her home. It all seemed anti-climactic, yet more than a little frightening. Was she safe here? Was she safe anywhere? Her world had blown apart. She wrapped an afghan around herself and collapsed on her couch. She was a wreck. The fact that her usually organized mind couldn't connect the dots of what had just happened terrified her.

An hour later, she was terrified all over again. She'd calmed down, realized that she was safe exactly as the deputy had said. And then she'd double-checked the contents of her purse and discovered that her artists' guild card with her picture, name and address was gone.

She'd had it when she'd left home. She'd intended to go to a local art gallery and discuss some of her latest works with them. For that, she needed the card. She usually had it in her wallet but today she'd been in a rush, known she'd be pulling it out shortly and had slipped the card into her purse and not into the wallet. Had it fallen out? Had the man who knocked her to the ground also picked up her artists' guild card? There'd been nothing on the sidewalk when she left. She'd double-checked. She could think of no other reason for its absence. Fear ran through her as she thought of the information he'd glean from the card.

She thought of calling the sheriff's office and asking for protection. But she knew what happened to people who witnessed a crime. And the law could only do so much. Now that the men who had robbed the bank knew who she was and where she lived, she wasn't safe. She couldn't wait for someone else to give lip service to the fact that they might help her.

Witnesses died. That was a fact. She'd lived her whole life knowing that terrible outcome. She couldn't wait. She couldn't depend on anyone else to protect her. She needed to get away until things cooled down.

Within an hour, she had a flight booked and was packing her things for the drive to Denver International Airport.

"I'll be back, and I'll give my testimony," she promised grimly as she locked the door of her house. And, she vowed as she gripped the wheel of her small pickup truck, not only would she live, but she'd make sure the jerk and his gang were put behind bars for the rest of their lives.

"YOU SCREWED THIS UP, you fix it!" snarled the man who liked to be called Evan. "Damn it, Luc, she saw you!"

Lucas Cruz held back the urge to slam his fist into Evan's taunting mouth. Evan had been the last to join the gang and even before this, he had been the proverbial thorn in Lucas's side. But there was no getting around it. Evan had seen the entire incident and he'd put the dots together. Because of that, he not only had to resolve a major screwup but he was being judged by the very men he'd led for the last few years.

"Not a problem," he snarled. "I'll fix it. Now, get out of my face before I—"

"Yeah, I'll get out of your face," Evan bristled. "When—"

"Shut the hell up," Rico broke in with a look of disdain at them both. "Lucas knows what has to be done. And we all know that the last thing we need is the cops on our tail. We're good now. But she opens her trap and it's all done." He glared at Lucas despite his words of support only seconds earlier. "I hope you have a plan."

"I'll deal with her. Meantime, carry on as planned," Lucas said with steel in his voice. He'd had enough. One more challenge from Rico and he'd take him out. That was what he'd thought only yesterday but now everything had changed and Rico knew it. "Get out of state. Go to Albuquerque and I'll meet you there. At the usual place. I know it's not ideal—"

"Hell," Rico snarled. "We could be caught because of your stupidity. She knows what you look like."

He was on Rico, his hands around his throat threatening to choke the life out of him. Someone had him from behind and pulled him off.

"It's over, Lucas, you don't call the shots on this

one," Rico said with a knife's edge to his voice. "Take Chen." He gave the young man a shove.

Lucas had to fight to cool the anger that ran hot and blistering through his veins. He had to fight not to kill Rico here and now. But those feelings would only get in the way of what he needed to do. Rico was right about one thing: he'd screwed up royally. It was him the witness had seen—no one else. This was the first time there'd been a witness who had seen one of their faces. His face.

He couldn't believe he'd screwed up so royally. He didn't know what he'd been thinking, or more accurately, not thinking. He'd thought nothing of it when he'd bumped into her on the street. She was a passerby, nothing more. She didn't know who he was or what he'd done or what he planned to do. Instead of on her, his mind had been on the heist.

The last place he had expected her to go was the same bank he was in the process of robbing. She'd been on the wrong side of the street for that. So was he, but that was part of how he entered any bank, from the opposite side. That upped the chances that anyone who might see him wouldn't connect him with the bank. He was also superstitious. He considered an approach from the opposite side to be lucky.

Their encounter had been an inconvenience— that was it. They'd bumped into each other and gone their separate ways. And now, she had to die for what she'd seen.

He grimaced. Bad luck had tailed him since the beginning of this robbery. To have the woman who'd gotten a clear view of him enter the bank in the midst of the robbery was the height of bad luck, or so he'd thought. But it got worse. The interruption allowed one of the tellers to set off the alarm. There'd been no time to do anything but get the hell out.

As a result, they'd run down a back alley, jumping into the nondescript SUV that had brought them there. By the time they were in motion, the sirens were shrill. The call had been too close, and it had all been downhill from there. They'd gotten away with a few thousand dollars, and only one step ahead of law enforcement. That was way too narrow of a getaway and too little of a take. The whole thing had been a fiasco from beginning to end.

She had no idea who he was, but she knew what he looked like. The authorities would soon have his face on file. Everything had looked grim until he'd remembered the card he'd picked up when her belongings had scattered on the sidewalk. He wasn't sure why he had done it—it might have been instinct. What it turned out was to be a bit of good luck. He had the witness's identity and her address. He'd had to wait until dark and even beyond that. It was around eleven, late enough that if the neighborhood wasn't asleep, it had mostly settled in for the night.

"Slow," he hissed in Spanish to the driver of the vehicle as they took the turn into the crescent where she lived.

"Here," he said a minute later. "Stop." They were half a block from her house.

He paused on the sidewalk. The few streetlights left the street shadowy and the houses in darkness. Despite that, he knew what the area was—he'd learned that immediately after finding her identity. It consisted of a middle-class group of mixed ethnicities, he thought with disdain. Some day he would buy and sell an area like this. Small cozy houses and neatly kept lawns as if the residents had nothing better to do than to monitor grass.

His hand dropped to his gun. It was there and ready. He hated being in this position. The only good thing was that they'd waited until dark. Most people had settled down for the night. No one would get a good look at them and if they did, they'd see Chen. Lucas was sending him in first.

He felt good about none of this. The only thing that was going to make him feel better was a bullet between the witness's pretty brown eyes. With that thought leading the way, he followed Chen. They'd go in through the back door. The alarm-warning sticker on her door meant nothing. The cheap door frame cracked when Chen shouldered it the first time and broke after the second. Nothing worried Lucas, not even the lights that he flicked recklessly on. They were masked and, as far as the alarm, by the time any monitoring agency reacted, they would be long gone.

But within minutes he knew one thing—she wasn't there. There was no vehicle in the driveway and the toiletries in her bathroom—the essentials anyway, like toothpaste and toothbrush—were missing.

He spewed a string of curses in Spanish. He always resorted to his native tongue when his emotions got the best of him. Time was running short. He sent his accomplice to check the living area while he moved to the kitchen. There, he saw his first sign of hope, a notepad on her kitchen counter. He went over and couldn't believe his luck. She'd written down flight information and it told him exactly what he needed to know. Two minutes later they'd left her neighborhood behind. Ten minutes after that, he was on the phone to his brother.

He explained the situation to him. "Are you in?" he asked and knew what the answer would be. His brother would do anything for money. That was why he was involved in one of the smaller Mexican drug cartels. He was counting on Yago's ties and his greed. He needed someone on her tail immediately. He needed someone in charge of catching her in Mexico and that someone was his brother, Yago.

"She won't get far. I know people who know people, if you know what I mean."

He did. He knew how the cartels worked and how they could find anyone. Or at least the bigger ones could. He had his doubts about the men his brother was linked with. They were brutal, but he wasn't too sure about their intel. What he did know was that right now, his brother and his connections were all he had. One way or another, she'd be found. He rolled the beads he always carried between the fingers of his right hand. They were lucky beads stolen from the hand of a dying woman.

He dropped the beads into his pocket. He hoped she'd savor her freedom, or for that matter, her life. Soon, all that would end.

Chapter Two

"What do you mean, you've lost her?" United States Marshal Trent Nielsen couldn't contain his frustration. Despite the fact that there'd been some interesting and complicated cases in his career that spanned a decade, this case was different. He knew the witness. It mattered like no case had mattered before. And he'd admit that to no one, not even to Jackson, a man he called friend. Going in, he'd been anxious to keep her safe—now it appeared she was far from that.

"Damn it, I should have been notified sooner." His impatience wasn't so much for the obvious reasons but something far more personal. Something that had had him volunteering for this assignment.

"Or what, this wouldn't have happened?" asked Jackson Vidal, federal agent. "No one could have predicted this." He raised an eyebrow. "Or is it something else that has your back up?"

"Having witness protection in place would have stopped her. You know it. This one's on you," Trent said. He took a breath. Anger couldn't change any of what had happened. He needed info and he needed to get on the road after her. What was done couldn't be undone.

Jackson leaned forward, his look dark, his eyebrows drawn together. "She disappeared before we could get her properly interviewed. At the time of the incident, she was in a state of panic and could remember little. If I'd been asked, I wouldn't have disagreed with the course of action. In hindsight, you're right, it was a screwup."

"More than a screwup. We have a witness who actually saw one of the thieves' faces unmasked." Trent shook his head. "What's the body count now for this gang?"

"Ten," Jackson said grimly. "Across two states and over as many months as there are bodies. But initially, the witness couldn't remember squat, she was so scared. That was the reason we put off getting her report until this morning. But when the deputy arrived with the sketch artist, the house had been broken into. Further investigation determined that she'd been gone before the break-in. She literally packed her bag and fled." He eyed Trent. "But you, you've got an inside scoop on the witness."

"Do I?" Trent asked but he knew exactly what Jackson meant. Still, he didn't want to reveal his true connection to Tara. He wanted Jackson to know as little as possible. The fact that they'd once been a couple might have him punted from the case as quickly as a slight connection had given him his in. His slight connection to the witness—they'd gone to the same high school. It was enough to give him an edge and be considered advantageous. Any more, and it might be considered trouble. Clearly, the fact that he'd once dated her had not come to light, for if it had, he would never have been assigned the case. And if it came to light, it would be considered detrimental and he could be pulled from the case. He hoped that never happened.

"You can't put much past me, Nielsen."

Trent met his dark gaze with one of his own. He wasn't sure how much Jackson knew.

"You went to high school together in Pueblo. At least for a year. And I'm guessing that's why you volunteered. You don't do much witness protection anymore. I was under the impression you dodged it when you could. So why this case over any other?" Jackson frowned and looked closely at Trent. "Is it all because you know her?"

"Partly," Trent agreed. It was true, he knew Tara or at least he'd known her as a girl. One thing was certain, he'd never forgotten her.

"Is she a friend?" Jackson asked.

"No," Trent said, knowing that kind of relationship could have him pulled from the case. But they weren't friends. They hadn't been in touch for years. "It's complicated."

"Uncomplicate me," Jackson said.

"I took her out a few times and then it fizzled," he admitted, knowing it was safer to reveal a scaled-down version of their relationship rather than try to get it all past Jackson.

"But you dated her?"

"Like I said, a few dates in high school." Tara. She'd caught his eye from the beginning. She'd been more mature for her years, at least to his seventeen-year-old self, she'd seemed so. Now he had nothing left but memories. Regrets that never left him.

He needed this assignment. He needed to find her and keep her safe like he hadn't all those years ago.

He met Jackson's doubting gaze. He hoped the truth didn't show in his face. That it had been more than a few dates, that he'd never forgotten her. Not that he held a torch for her; it was nothing like that. He'd gone on with his life, dated other women and was currently solidly single and happy.

But Jackson wouldn't believe that Trent's volunteering for this assignment didn't mean something else. Jackson was cynical that way, which might be why he was still a bachelor. He didn't understand that you could care for someone without being in a relationship.

Trent pushed the thoughts from his mind. None of that mattered. What mattered was Tara and keeping her safe.

While they hadn't spoken in the years since she left Pueblo, he knew where she'd been and much of what had happened to her. He knew that she'd returned to Pueblo after taking classes toward a general arts degree with a minor in admin from a state university. He knew, too, that she'd never finished that degree. He knew a lot more than he wanted to admit.

"Unfortunately, none of that is relevant. Due to the fact that she's on the run, we need a change in protocol. What we need," Jackson said, staring Trent down, "is someone who can get inside her head. Fortunately, she didn't cover her tracks well. We were able to learn where she was headed from the note left by her phone. She took a flight from Denver to Mexico City." He looked at his smartwatch. "She should have landed over six hours ago."

"I don't like the sound of any of this. Old-school as a bank robbery is, these people have proved to be vicious. They've left a trail of bodies across two states in the last year. And there's nothing to say they weren't the ones who broke in looking for her."

"Exactly. And they're still on the loose. As far as Tara goes, we're finalizing the setup of a safe house," Jackson said. "I will send you the details once it's complete. Unfortunately, we have no witness to put there."

"I'll rectify that," Trent said with determination. But fear rode in his gut. She was alone and in Mexico with a killer who could be hot on her trail. And if he wasn't, there could be contacts, people deployed— unknowns. He was in a race to find Tara.

"Let's get you on a flight out. Your history may make it easier to establish trust with her," Jackson said. "That is, once you locate her."

"I'll find her," Trent said as if to reinforce the confidence Jackson had in him.

"I'm counting on it. I've a moratorium on body bags. This gang has to be shut down—fast. This has been a bad year for murders. I don't need these yahoos carrying on and making it worse than it already is."

Trent nodded but he was buried in his thoughts about how effective he was going to be. The wild card was Tara. The last time he'd seen her, she'd been in tears. Then he'd considered it unnecessary drama. He'd acted like a typical teenage boy—without empathy, without much feeling of any kind. He'd turned his back on her tears but not before telling her that she was acting like a baby.

Despite his youth at the time, the memory still disturbed him. It was his one regret in life. Her tears were ones that he had caused. On hearing that her family was moving, instead of comforting her and offering ways that they could remain in touch, he'd broken up with her. It had been a completely defensive reaction. Walking away, acting macho had somehow cloaked his own hurt.

He wished he could go back and tell that self that he needed to grow up. He wished that he could have prevented the whole scene. Prevented everything that happened to her immediately after.

But at the time, he had been too busy hiding his feelings when he'd heard that she was moving. Too busy trying to be tough to realize the pain he had caused her. He hadn't understood what he was losing when he'd thought it wise to break up rather than go long-distance. And then it had all gotten worse when her father had been shot by someone assumed to be criminally involved with the very suspect he was to testify against.

But that was the past. He could see why Tara had run. She had a bad history with authorities. She was walking proof that the law couldn't always do what it promised. Her father was promised protection, and he'd believed. Now he was dead.

She'd not be happy to see Trent. The last thing she'd said to him was that she'd never forgive him. They'd been young then but the words haunted him even now. They were words that told him she'd have none of his presence shadowing her and that she wouldn't be apt to take his counsel.

What she'd need to know was that there was no choice. He was her shadow until this was over. He'd keep her safe. He could only hope to hell that she stayed safe until he found her.

His thoughts flipped to the threat. This group was as yesteryear as it was violent. Bank robberies were passé. It was only the number and violence associated with their crimes that was taking them up the ladder of Most Wanted. The fact that there'd not only been a witness in their latest robbery, but they'd gone after her changed everything. The break-in at her house, combined with the fact that the witness had disappeared, had turned the case on its head.

He thought of how gutsy she was, returning to live alone in Pueblo, forging ahead with her life. Not only that, but she'd come face-to-face with a bank robber. Now she was alone and confronting a danger no civilian should have to. He had to find her and quickly.

"By the way, if you hadn't volunteered, I would have asked for you," Jackson said. "You might not like witness protection, but you haven't failed once. We've lost no witnesses under your watch. And this—I admit, I hesitated because of the personal connection. I'd hate to see—"

"Like you said," Trent interrupted. "I haven't lost a witness yet and I won't start now."

"The file is fairly concise right up until she boarded that damn plane," Jackson said.

Trent nodded. He'd read it. She'd driven to Denver, and from there she'd boarded a flight to Mexico City. That was where her trail dead-ended.

"You had her in the palm of your hand. Now she could be anywhere," he said, annoyed that she hadn't been stopped, that this hadn't been foreseen. "Why wasn't she offered witness protection immediately?"

"There was no indication that she would run. She was in her own community, her own house. The thought was that she was safe, that we had time—if needed—to get witness protection in place. The perps were believed to have left town, as they always do. And there's no evidence that didn't happen."

"Except in the case where they hunted down two witnesses before ever leaving the area." He referenced a robbery that had occurred recently in Fort Collins, Colorado.

"That was within minutes of the robbery and just outside the bank."

"But it happened," Trent said darkly, not liking

any part of what he was hearing. "And this time, they were after her. Damn it!"

"There's no proof of that," Jackson said.

"That was what frightened her."

"That was our initial thought but that wasn't the case. She was gone long before the break-in. Her flight reservation was made in the early hours of the afternoon. Unfortunately, that information was on her kitchen counter. It was fair game for anyone in her house."

"Unbelievable," Trent said.

"We've got what little we could gather from the neighbors," Jackson continued. "A dog was barking around eleven o'clock last night. A neighbor looked out and saw a strange car cruising the area. She thought she saw two men but no description." He shrugged. "It wasn't enough to put in an emergency call and she let the incident go unreported."

"You're thinking the guy Tara can identify came after her?"

"Possibly, but that's only speculation." Jackson pushed the file aside. "Something else. Years ago, her father was killed while in witness protection. He witnessed a notorious drug dealer shoot a rival gang member. We had him in witness protection. It was to no avail. Two months later he was shot crossing a street and pronounced dead at the scene."

"Doesn't give her much trust that the system will be there for her," Trent said.

"No, it doesn't. But I don't know why I'm repeating this. You knew all that," Jackson said and shrugged as if that didn't matter. "Add to that the fact that no one spoke to her about protection of any kind." He smacked the desk. "By the time we sent a man to interview her, it was clear that someone else had been there first. The back door had been broken in. And the porch door was open. Interesting thing was that there was nothing taken. At least that's what we assume, as everything was in place."

"I can see why she might have run but son of a—" Trent bit off the expletive. "This makes things difficult."

"Between us, we'll get her back," Jackson said.

"Us?" Trent repeated with just a hint of sarcasm.

"You," Jackson stated with finality.

Ten hours later

IT HAD ALL sounded so easy then. But it was early morning the next day before Trent was on the last leg of his journey to Mexico City. An hour before the plane landed, he called Enrique Gonzales. Despite the time, the second in command of the Mexican Federal Police was already up and on his second cup of coffee. An hour after the plane landed, Trent was in a cab and heading for the coffee bar Enrique had suggested for them to meet at.

"I've found nothing," Enrique said with a grim look. "We know she landed here. We know that it was a late-afternoon flight. She didn't rent a car at the airport. We interviewed everyone in the vicinity. Only the man at the concession stand had any information. He got the impression that she wasn't planning to stay long, at least not in Mexico City." He shook his head. "Don't forget the guy's grasp of English is poor to say the least. He could have misunderstood. So, other than that, there's nothing. But you know how it is. That's the downfall of a city this large. There's too many people, even the tourists disappear into the chaos." He shrugged. "That doesn't mean that I've given up. That's the status for now."

Trent nodded. Everything that Enrique was saying made sense. Coming down here was a long shot. Now he wondered if he'd been overly optimistic in thinking that finding her might be that easy.

"Anyway, I did a little more digging based on what you told me," Enrique said. "The fact that she's an artist got my interest and also got me thinking. Now, this is only a guess. But I wondered, would she go to San Miguel de Allende?"

Trent wasn't surprised to hear the name. It was a popular haunt for many in the arts community. "She's been there before. Twice. I saw it on her Facebook feed from a few years ago." In fact, he'd done a search on the city on the flight here, thinking that it might be a possibility. She'd been a gifted artist as a girl. But it was a clue that might have struck gold.

"The arts community is tight. Someone there may know something. I'd say it's worth a shot."

"I planned to search here first," Trent said. "There's no guarantee that she's left Mexico City."

"Good point, but we can save time if I keep my

nose to the ground here and you check out San Miguel. If I find anything, I'll let you know."

"Sounds like a plan," he said. "Thanks, man."

An hour later, Trent was heading for a car rental agency. Whether Tara was in San Miguel de Allende or whether she was somewhere else in Mexico was anyone's guess. The only thing he knew for sure was that she hadn't boarded another plane out of Mexico City.

Chapter Three

Tara leaned back on the ornate white metal chair that was already well warmed by the morning sun. She was in a small courtyard that faced the main cobbled street where vendors congregated. The courtyard fronted the arched alcove of the heritage building. It was there where she'd rented a tiny apartment. The landlords—Carlos and his wife, Francesca—specialized in housing artistic types from all over the world. Their rates were good, or in better terms cheap. She'd stayed there before on her last visits. But this time around it seemed empty and worn and more than a little sad. Things seemed a little more run-down, like business hadn't been so good.

She watched as a stooped and withered woman wheeled a wagon full of red, yellow and blue baskets down the street. The wheel of the barrow bounced on the cobblestones. A young boy ran behind her, dashing to one side and then the other.

Tara smiled as she leaned forward, watching the scene, taking in the details. She held a sketching pencil in one hand, and a strand of blond hair slipped free of the braid that hung down her back. From the first moment she'd discovered San Miguel de Allende, she'd felt at home. Even now, after all that had happened, she felt safe.

The place she rented was in the heart of the city. Here, one historic building after another butted against each other. The city was founded in the early-sixteenth century and much of the architecture from that time still existed.

She glanced over and caught a glimpse of Siobhan O'Riley coming out a side door. Siobhan worked in the small café that was part of the property and run by her landlords. Tara had met her on her first visit to the city and since then, they'd stayed in touch. On that visit, when Tara had left to go home, Siobhan had stayed, putting down roots and swearing that she'd never return to the rains of Ireland.

"Here's your coffee," Siobhan said. "With a touch of milk. Toast. Butter and jam on the side." She set the breakfast down.

"Thanks." Tara closed her sketchbook and put her pencil down.

"You here for long this time?"

"I'm not sure," she said, unable to hide the pensive note she knew was in her voice. She was running on cash and she wasn't sure what she was going to do when that ran out. There was a lot she didn't know, like the legalities of working here should she need to. But if staying meant finding a job, whether it was legitimate or under-the-table, she'd do it. She'd do whatever it took.

The memories of what she'd witnessed haunted her sleep and potentially threatened her life. Money seemed such a small thing in comparison. She had bigger things to worry about, like not being found, possibly changing her name. Eventually, she knew she'd go home and testify. When it was safe, when she was needed, just not now.

Tara ate her toast as she watched the activity on the street. Sellers' stalls lined the street for as far as she could see. The smell of cooking food filled the air. She reached down to scratch the ear of her landlords' small dog. He was a true mutt, so mixed that she wasn't sure what breed might dominate.

"Ah, Maxx, if only every man were like you. Adoring and patient," she said with a laugh and another scratch behind his ears. A door opened. The dog turned.

She waved at Francesca, who gave her a smile and waved back. She felt safe here, the older couple who owned the rental units were kind, and it made her feel safe to know that Carlos was a retired police inspector.

"Maxx," Francesca called. The dog got to his feet and ran toward her.

Tara had to laugh at the speed the dog moved. She guessed that it might be mealtime. Her smile stayed as her attention went back to the bustle of commerce on the street just below her. For the courtyard was raised above the street level by a flight of stone steps. It was a busy and entertaining sight. The colors alone could keep one's attention. The awnings over the storefronts and the vendors' stalls were numerous hues, all of them vibrant. They added to the collage that was only enhanced by the merchandise. Color was the theme reflected everywhere.

She loved the market. Each of the vendors had their stories if you had time to listen. The first time she'd been here, she'd celebrated her thirtieth birthday. That had been four years ago. The event had felt huge as if her entire life had shifted. Birthdays were about that, but getting out of her twenties had her considering what it was she was dedicating her life to. It was a strange and too-serious thought for a birthday celebrated on a vacation in Mexico.

Despite the serious thoughts, she'd had fun. It was the youthful fun and her first taste of adventure that had fed her artistic side and made it so easy to bring out a feeling in a painting.

She'd come back again one year later but that trip had been very different. She'd been recovering from the tragic end to a relationship.

She should have broken up with Mark months before but he'd been persistent that they were made for each other. She'd never been too sure. Mark had been steady. He had liked to say he was her rock. But he was also dull and for the last months before the car crash that had killed him, she'd flirted with breaking up with him. When he'd died and the ring had been found, she'd known that he was about to propose and that only made the guilt of her true feelings that much more difficult to bear.

After his death, a trip to San Miguel de Allende

had been an escape. In a way it had freed her from
the guilt that plagued her. She'd met others like her,
some she'd met the year before, all people involved
in the arts in some way. It had been the best place to
heal and to begin to celebrate life again.

She took a last swallow of coffee and got up, heading down the street to get a closer look at the vendors'
goods. She could almost trick herself into believing that this was a vacation, that she wasn't here
because she was afraid for her life. She wondered
when it would be safe to return and how she would
ever know if and when that was.

She pushed the thoughts away as she checked out
a produce vendor and then a number of vendors with
handicrafts. She admired a vividly hand-painted bag
from another vendor. The vibrancy of the bag and
the fact that it was hand done made it almost impossible to resist. But her money situation put that internal debate to rest. She still had a beautiful bag she'd
purchased on that first trip four years ago. She left
the vendor with a smile of admiration.

After an hour, she decided to head back to her
room, but a block away she sensed something was
off. Her intuition had been bang on since she was
a child. It was something she'd inherited from her
mother, or at least so her mother claimed. She could
sense change.

She could only pray that what she was sensing
was a change for the better. She wasn't sure she could
handle worse.

TRENT HUMMED A popular song he'd heard half a dozen times since he'd landed. Except for getting out of Mexico City's chaos, it had been an easy drive to San Miguel de Allende. It was a relief to be on the open road without a lot of traffic. After the insanity of a city the size of Mexico's capital, this was a balm to his soul. He'd bought a Coke midway at a dusty little store on the edges of a village whose name he'd already forgotten. He'd hit the outskirts of San Miguel de Allende shortly after lunch.

The city was gorgeous even from its outer edges, where the beauty of its historical architecture surpassed everything he could imagine. There wasn't the usual ugly industrial area or bland box stores fringing the outskirts like one might see in other cities. That didn't surprise him. He'd done his research on the flight from Denver. But even with a heads-up, the history of the city was amazing, not just preserved in a plethora of century's old architecture, but vibrant, almost alive.

The red spires of a church seemed to push through the cluster of stone that, from what he could see from the outskirts, made up the center of the town. He passed a more modern inn with a waterslide and, just behind that, another heritage stone church. His plan was to get as close to the city center as possible before parking. That was what Enrique had recommended after stating that the streets were narrow and congested.

Twenty minutes later, Trent learned that Enrique

knew what he was talking about. The streets were tight and crowded with an assortment of pedestrians and vendors. He'd already hiked past a half dozen vendors, a man with a donkey and a trio of stray dogs.

He needed to find people who fitted the profile in his head. People who might have spoken to Tara. He needed to ask them questions that would help him find her. But the vendors seemed too caught up in their transactions and he'd have to queue up to get near any of them.

He began his queries at the first outdoor café where a couple sat sipping coffee. Trent guessed he'd have better luck here, speaking to people like these, people like Tara. People who had more in common with her, as artists and foreigners. That group stuck together here in this town. There was a whole enclave and a new member to that group would be news. They'd be the ones who might be familiar with a beautiful young artist from Colorado.

With that in mind, he saw a woman with a pencil in her hand and a sketching pad in front of her. Her partner's Hawaiian-themed T-shirt was only a bonus. They were as good a place to start as any.

It was on the sixth try that he hit the jackpot. The woman he asked had not only heard of Tara but she had spoken to her only an hour ago. Within minutes, he was heading toward the sun-faded red stone building where the woman had directed him.

He couldn't believe it had been this easy. He always felt that easy meant trouble. He walked along the uneven and narrow cobblestone street. It was crowded with merchants, shoppers and even the occasional donkey. As he did, he worried that there was something he had missed.

Five minutes later, he stopped on the edge of a yellow brick building at the junction of two streets. He saw the long blond hair first. It streamed freely down her back. He headed in that direction, going up a short flight of stairs to a small courtyard with a half dozen white metal tables and chairs to where the blond-haired woman was wiping a table.

"Excuse me," he said.

She turned but it wasn't Tara and disappointment bit deep.

"I was looking for Tara Munroe," he began.

"Tara," the woman said with a bright lilt to her voice. She held out her hand, her eyes alight with an admiration that was impossible to miss. "Siobhan."

He gave her the briefest of handshakes and didn't offer his name.

"Is she here?"

The smile she gave him was slightly flirtatious, but her eyes went somewhere over his shoulder.

"Tara," Siobhan called. "Someone to see you."

He felt someone else, someone watching from behind. He turned as a door leading away from the common area swung open and another blonde stood there. But this one was familiar.

He knew those high cheekbones. He knew that slightly rounded face. And he knew the dark brown eyes that now held a combination of curiosity and fear. He'd know that face anywhere. He'd looked at it enough times during the flight here, and he'd remembered the girl she'd been, of course. Still, he was stunned by the woman she'd become.

She gave an air of both confidence and fragility. She had matured into a soulful combination of beauty and innocence. If he'd been able to paint at all, he'd paint her, he'd…

She'd been the one who painted, not him.

Siobhan moved around him, standing slightly to his left as she looked from one to the other.

"You know each other?"

He couldn't take his eyes off Tara.

"Trent," Tara murmured.

His name on her lips was like a seductive whisper. He felt frozen in time. He stared at her, noticing how her hair moved in the light breeze. She was staring back. She looked shocked, as if she couldn't believe what she was seeing. He couldn't blame her. After all, he'd arrived on her doorstep, a memory of her past, without warning.

She looked at him as if seeing him for the first time. "Is it really you?"

"It is," he said and only wanted to hug her, to touch her. To tell her how sorry he was to have left her the way he had all those years ago. He'd apologized for none of that. Even when her father had died, he hadn't contacted her. Now he stood and waited for her to decide on what the next move would be. He wondered if the past could be redone whether he would have done any better.

She took a step forward. Her beautiful brown eyes were dark, almost stormy, like she sensed trouble. "What are you doing here? Why—"

He glanced at Siobhan. He didn't want to admit why he was there. Not in front of the woman who seemed determined to protect her.

"It's all right, Siobhan," Tara said. "You can leave us alone to talk. I know him."

As Siobhan left, he pulled out a chair for Tara.

"I can't believe you're here and I can't imagine why," she said as she accepted the seat he offered.

"I'm a US marshal," he said.

Her face became pale beneath her light tan. "Like you always wanted to be," she whispered.

"I did, didn't I," he said with some relief at the temporary diversion.

She laced her fingers and her lips pinched together. She refused to meet his eyes as she asked, "Why are you here, Trent?"

"You witnessed a bank robbery in Pueblo, Colorado." This time it was his official voice speaking.

She looked at him with eyes that seemed weary and doubtful at the same time. Their sheen only reminded him of all she'd been through. He was grateful that he'd put himself forward for this. Grateful that it was him here and not someone else who didn't know her as he did. Seeing her like this only told him that she needed him.

"Tara." He reached over and took one of her hands in both of his. Her palm was clammy. It was as if the very mention of what had happened, what she had run from, threw her into an immediate panic. He hoped that he was wrong, that his assessment was off but...

"I can't believe they sent you all the way here," she said in a voice that was tired, drained even.

The act of keeping it together seemed to have slipped, like she was too tired to care. He was glad of that. Playing games would only lengthen the process. He wanted to fast-track this and get her home, where he had more resources.

"There wasn't a choice," he said, pushing his thoughts aside.

"What do you mean?"

"You're the only witness. Which means that you could put a notorious bank robber behind bars."

"I know but I'm scared. After what happened to my dad." She took a breath. "He had police security assigned."

"A marshal," he corrected.

"And it didn't matter. He was the witness that could put a drug dealer away and he was shot in public." Her voice choked off and it was a moment to regain her control.

He waited, knowing that there was nothing he could do or say that would change any of it.

"I just know that I'm safe here."

"No, Tara, you're not."

"I don't like where this is going," she said.

"It was a mistake to run, Tara. You're safer at

home, under my protection. Your testimony will be needed should this ever go to trial. And…"

She was shaking her head. He tried not to be mesmerized by those dark soulful eyes that saw everything, or so it seemed. He'd forgotten that about her. As he'd grown up and forged an adult life, there were things he didn't want to remember. But now with her here, no longer a memory and with her eyes fixed on him, he couldn't look away. He remembered everything about her, eclipsing what he'd forgotten. He pulled his thoughts back to reality, to the situation and not the girl he'd once thought he'd loved. That girl was now a woman he had to protect.

"I'm flattered that you took on this assignment, Trent, but it wasn't necessary."

Her look said that because she knew him, she also knew what he was about. Some of that was true. But if that was what she thought, she had a whole lot wrong—dangerously wrong.

"Flattered?" He bit back a knot of anger. What the hell was she saying? She thought he did this out of kindness or some misguided gesture of goodwill? "There's men who will kill you for what you saw."

Her face lost what color it had. "That's why I'm here, Trent. Where no one can find me. I'll stay until this all blows over and then I'll go home and give my testimony."

"It's not going to blow over. You need—"

"I don't need your protection, not here. I'm far enough away. I'll be safe."

"Tara…"

"No, Trent." She looked distraught.

On the nearby street, a guitar began to softly chord a melody that was as strange as it was beautiful. He glanced over and saw a man sitting with his back against the dusty red stone wall of a building, one leg stretched out as he played his guitar. In another situation, it would be romantic.

He turned his attention from the guitarist and to Tara. He needed her cooperation and he needed it quickly. There was no time to mince words. And yet, contradictorily, he didn't want to frighten her. She'd been through enough but… The thought broke off. She needed to know. He had to tell her to keep her safe.

"You're in danger. Mexico might be another country, but despite that, you didn't run far enough."

"What do you mean?"

"Someone broke into your house after you left, Tara. We can only assume that they saw the same note we did. Your flight information was easy to find, left on the kitchen counter."

"Someone? What do you mean? What are you implying?"

He brought his hand flat on the table. "Damn it, Tara. Do you have any idea your value dead?"

"No." Her voice was barely a whisper.

"The stakes are high, Tara. These thieves have a lot to lose. If they take you out, they keep the money, their freedom and carry on with their crime spree. Essentially, they profit from your death." He paused, hating the brutal truth to his words. "We won't let that happen. That's why I'm here."

"They found me?" her voice was soft.

"There's no indication of that," he said.

"What if they do?"

"Then I do my job. I keep you alive."

Chapter Four

"I thought running was enough," Tara said and her voice trembled. Her fingers were interlaced in front of her as if that would keep her steady.

"I'm sorry, Tara. I know that was harsh. And no, it wasn't that you didn't run far enough, it was that you tried to do it alone. The truth is that you're a witness who could threaten a man's freedom. You can't put a price on that."

Trent regretted laying the facts out so bluntly. But he desperately needed to get her to see how grave the situation was and how much she needed him.

"At home it's different—I can protect you more easily. I have more resources and I can carry a gun."

"Back to Pueblo?"

"Not necessarily. Definitely the States," he said. "Witness protection is being set up. I came after you before getting the details on where you'd be located. You'll be in witness protection until the trial is over."

She shook her head as a tremor seemed to run through her.

"Think about it, about going home to the States."

He paused. "With me," he finished. "I know you just got here but this was a mistake. Running was a mistake."

"Just like my dad," she said. Sadness was like a heavy film running through her voice.

"Not like him at all, Tara." Her father had been killed, shot while under witness protection. He cringed at the thought of how that had all come down. His killer had never seen justice.

"I'm sorry, Tara. I can't change the past but I guarantee you this, you'll be safe. I'll keep you safe." He took her hands. "I promise." And he knew that he'd keep that promise or die trying.

She pulled her hands free. "No one can make that kind of promise. Not even you, Trent."

He skipped over her doubt. "Like I said, I can offer you more protection at home. These men are violent criminals and they'll do everything they can to prevent being caught." He looked her in the eye. "You're the one thing standing between them and their freedom and they may know you're in Mexico."

He didn't know how often he had to repeat it. But their window of time was unknown. He wanted her home where he could ensure her safety. Not here, in a country that he wasn't unfamiliar with but one where he couldn't even carry arms. The sooner he got her home the better.

"I'm far enough away. And I'm only a concern to one of them."

"Maybe. But your testimony could put the one we suspect to be the leader behind bars. Just one of them standing trial will jeopardize the others. You're the key to ending one of the most successful gangs of armed robbers in recent years. There's also the possibility of a domino effect. Them turning on each other. In that case, you could put them all behind bars. They've killed for money, I don't think killing for their freedom would be a stretch." He was going for the shock factor now. He needed her to get on board with going home and he needed her to do it quickly.

He'd give her a day, two at the outside. She'd see things his way soon enough. For now, it wasn't a bad decision to spend a couple more days than he planned. Inconvenient for him but it was something that could have her more solid in her decision than if he rushed her back. He'd roll with it, but he had one more tool in his arsenal.

Before he could say anything more, however, Siobhan brought out a coffee for each of them.

Trent had to fight to hide his impatience. He'd made an impact on Tara and an interruption was the last thing he needed. Besides that, he'd been going in fast-forward since he'd been assigned the case.

But as he glanced at Tara, he realized how selfish his thoughts were. He was thinking in terms of the end result, not in terms of how this was affecting her. She was safe enough for now. They had time—not a lot, but more than he'd initially allowed for. His being here is shock enough. He reminded himself that as usual, he was coming on too strong. But it was like a clock was ticking in his head. He needed to take a step back. It was clear in the fact that she had run in the first place that she more than realized the danger she was in. His immediate task was to convince her that she couldn't do it on her own. He had found her and that only made it clear to him that the scuzbag who might be coming after her could find her, too. She needed not just him but the resources that backed him.

"Thanks, Siobhan. I can never get enough. There's nothing better than a good cup of coffee in the moring."

"Thanks," Trent said only because it was expected. In reality he had no desire for coffee. Caffeine was something he didn't want. But he took the cup. He might not drink it, but he could not ignore the gesture.

"How's it going?" Siobhan asked.

"Fine," Tara said. "Trent is an old friend. From high school," she said with a grimace. "We've kept in touch. Although, I sure didn't expect to find him here but—"

"But here he is," Trent added, impressed with her bit of improv. Maybe this would work out better than he thought. "We follow each other on social media."

He could feel Tara's gaze on him.

He glanced over at her and an understanding seemed to pass between them. For what he'd said was a flat-out lie.

Siobhan looked doubtful, but she didn't ask any questions.

"How's it with you?" Tara asked. "Any better?"

Sioban shrugged. "No. Like I said the other day, the place is near empty much of the time. I'm not sure why they keep me on. Not only that, but I saw Carlos turn down potential renters more than once. I've heard him and Francesca fight about it and I have absolutely no idea what's going on but it's not making this job look too secure."

Tara turned to Trent. "That's sure changed since the last time I was here. In fact, I wasn't sure that I wouldn't be turned away, they were so busy."

"No chance of that now," Siobhan said before returning to work.

"Have a drink with us this evening," Tara said to her.

Trent had to bite back his surprise and disappointment. She was putting a buffer in place. It was the oldest trick in the book.

"Sure," Siobhan said with an appreciative look at Trent.

"Okay," Tara said. "Gloria's Vino and Tacos at seven."

A minute later a phone rang and Siobhan headed inside.

Shortly after that, a man who Trent pegged to be approximately sixty came out of the main house. His taller-than-average height and heavier build half hid the thin woman behind him until she moved slightly ahead of him. The woman's high-heeled sandals and sundress, and his pale blue cotton pants and golf shirt completed a put-together look that made it clear they were going out.

The man's dark eyes seemed to rake over Trent. But it wasn't just a look, it was an assessment, an analyzing of who he was or who he might be.

"Carlos, Francesca, this is my friend Trent. Trent, my landlords." Tara paused as they shook hands and exchanged a few pleasantries.

"He's here for a few days."

"Where are you staying?" Francesca asked.

Trent didn't look at Tara for he didn't know what her reaction would be to what he was about to say. But now that he was here, there was no way he was not going to do his job and protect her. That meant being nearby. "I thought I'd bunk on Tara's couch. A night or two," he clarified.

He could almost feel her outrage. But to her credit, she said nothing.

He didn't look at her but instead addressed the one thing that he was sure would be uppermost in her landlords' minds—rent.

"I'll pay…"

"No," Carlos said. "I'm not charging for a few days on a hard couch. If you stay longer than that, we'll work a deal."

Carlos's words seemed casual but despite that, Trent felt like he was under a spotlight in the way Carlos looked at him. He seemed to see through him as if he knew a secret about him, as if… The thought trailed off but not his suspicions about Carlos. He wasn't a regular civilian despite his looks, dress and current profession. There was a look of assurance about him combined with cynicism that Trent had seen before and that piqued his interest.

"You're sure you'll be comfortable on her couch?" Francesca asked.

"We have rooms available," Carlos said.

"I…" He squeezed Tara's hand as she began to speak. He guessed that finally, she was about to contradict him. He leaned over and kissed her full on the lips. He didn't have time to think about what he did or how it impacted her. He was just trying to swing things his way.

The kiss was short and his attention was just as quickly turned to the couple, who were now officially his landlords.

"Empty rooms because you refuse to advertise." Francesca looked at Carlos with a frown.

Carlos laid a hand on his wife's shoulder. "We've already talked about this, Frannie," he said with a tone of gentle resignation. He turned his attention back to Trent and Tara.

"We'd visit with you," Carlos said. "But Frannie and I will be late for the show."

"What do you mean you're staying on my couch?" Tara asked a minute later when the couple were gone. "You're kidding me. We're long over, Trent."

"It's not about that," he said patiently. "I don't think you understand the seriousness of this. Your life could be in danger, even here. What you saw… These men could come after you. We can't take the chance that whoever broke into your house isn't tied to that robbery. If it was, they have your travel information, Tara. They know where you are."

Her hand stopped in midair with the cup in her hand. She'd admitted an addiction to coffee only a few hours ago. He remembered her comment that had tailed the admission.

THERE'S NOTHING BETTER than a good cup of coffee in the morning.

Now she set the cup down with a bang. Coffee sloshed over the edge of the cup, but her eyes remained on him. "You think they'd find me here?" Panic etched her words.

"It's a possibility, Tara. We can't discount it." He covered her hand with his. "I don't mean to frighten you but whether that's the case or not, you're a major threat. You saw one of their faces. That could put him in jail for a long time. Of course, they would have to know where you lived."

"Oh no." Her hand gripped his wrist as if the very touch would give her strength. "When my things dropped out of my purse that day, I lost my artists' guild card."

"What!"

"My things scattered onto the sidewalk and I lost my guild card. It had my picture, my address—everything he'd need to find me. And he was right there when I dropped it." She looked at him with terror in her eyes. "That's why I couldn't stay. There was no way it was safe. They know who I am and you're suggesting that there's a chance they know where I am?"

Her hand flung sideways. The coffee cup fell over, sending the remains of her coffee across the table. Both of them ignored the trail of liquid that dripped off the edge. Their eyes were locked on each other.

He didn't know what to say, not at first. What she'd said shocked him. It could bring the worst-case scenario to fruition. Her lips were pinched and her whole demeanor was troubled and yet there was something in the way she looked at him, in the way she no longer looked ready to bolt, that he hoped hinted at trust.

But the reality was that she also looked like she might be sick. "I was in such a rush." She looked at him with a mixture of sorrow and fear. "I played the odds and unfortunately, I was right. They found my home." Her lips trembled.

He nodded. Not that he agreed with her action, but he could understand why she'd run. He wasn't so sure that in the same circumstance, without a law enforcement background, that he might not have done the same, or at least considered it. It didn't matter whether he agreed or not. Now he had to ensure her safety and to do that he needed her to be in complete agreement that she needed his protection.

"It was bad timing," he said. "Fortunately, nothing was taken and the house wasn't trashed. That leads to the conclusion that they were looking for something specific, or someone. That they were looking for you."

Her hands were clenched in front of her and she looked more frightened now than anything else.

"I plan to bring you home, to a safe house, without delay."

He knew his mistake as soon as he saw her look of panic. She wasn't ready to be pushed this hard. It didn't matter what she now knew—it wasn't enough. She needed what little time he could give her to let reality set in. He'd seen witnesses react like this before, like the truth was overwhelming when provided all at once. Sometimes it had to be fed to them in small pieces, bit by bit, and then they needed what little time could be offered to digest their situation.

"No, Trent. No, I won't go. Not yet." She shook her head. "You're wrong."

Cripes, he thought. What did she need? Her denial was too adamant. He needed her buy-in, or at least the start of a buy-in. "They saw your travel itinerary. If it was anyone associated with the robbery, they'd know you're in Mexico. It would be that easy."

She folded her arms and there was a set to her chin that wasn't there before.

"They'll find you, Tara. Maybe not today or tomorrow, but if they want you bad enough—"

"But they don't know I'm here in San Miguel de Allende. Mexico is a big country."

"Don't they? A mention of San Miguel de Allende being an artist mecca was all it took for me to remember that you'd been here before—twice. I saw that on your social media feed posted three and four years ago. I found both references to San Miguel. That's wiped now but anyone else could have seen it. They could guess that in Mexico you might return to a place that was familiar."

"I never thought of that. I—"

"And now if they have your flight itinerary…" He let the sentence drop, let her reach her own conclusions.

"If…" But there was little resistance in the word.

"Mexico City was easy. You gave that one away. It's clear you don't know what you're doing and that is going to spell trouble. They'll find you."

He paused, locking into those brown eyes that even in this situation seemed to do something to him. They made him more aware of her as a woman and not the girl he had long left behind. He took her hands, squeezing them between his.

"There are two options here."

"Don't give me an ultimatum." There was anger in her eyes and a shake to her voice. "This is all just speculation. Besides, like I said, Mexico is a big country."

He remembered that about her. How she'd use anger as a shield. "Not big enough," he said.

Her eyes were huge in her pale face.

He knew that despite her bravado she was very afraid. He felt bad. He didn't want her afraid, but he needed her to know that eventually, home was exactly where he'd take her. He also knew this was a lot thrown at her all at once. He needed to give her time. Still, he kept pushing.

"You come home with me now or, like I said and I've already got your landlords' approval, I sleep on your couch until I convince you otherwise. Your choice."

"Damn you, Nielsen," she said as she got up and turned to walk away. "The couch is all yours. Have at her because I'm sure as hell not going home."

"Not yet," he said in an undertone to her retreating back. "But soon."

He chuckled as she turned around and gave him a bright smile and a sign that told him exactly where he could go. For a second, he felt like he'd hit Rewind and they were back in Pueblo so many years ago.

If only he could go there. Back to the past would be the safest place of all. Before this, before the tragedy, before any of it. A time when life had been innocent kisses and promises of forever love.

It was a time that would never return and one that he would never forget.

Chapter Five

The next morning, Tara woke up earlier than usual. What little sleep she'd gotten had been broken by troubling dreams. She'd finally drifted off in the early hours. She was troubled at Trent's presence as much as she was by the nightmare that he'd so recently resurrected. Him being here, him finding her, had completely thrown her. What he'd told her had terrified her. As a result, she'd had one horrifying dream after another.

Thoughts of him had kept her awake the majority of the night. He still made her heart race, but in a different way than he had all those years ago. She'd had to stop herself from staring at his confident stance as he stood taking in the activity in the street, or noticing how his hair curled dark and rich over his collar.

This was not the boy she had left behind when her family had moved all those years ago. She hadn't seen him since he was seventeen and there was no comparison. His physique was that of a man who worked out. His manner was poised. He was a man used to winning and that both frightened and attracted her. And still she stumbled on memories of the past.

She remembered it all. She'd never forgotten. Six months out of their life—she'd been fifteen and he'd been seventeen. He'd been her first love, part of the magic of Pueblo. It was what made Pueblo different, and because of that, the city had lured her back.

She smiled as details of their relationship flooded back to her. They'd been so young, so naive. She remembered talking with him for hours, lying on their backs in the park, sharing their dreams and aspirations. He'd wanted to be in law enforcement. She'd never doubted him. But she'd never thought that one day he would not only succeed but become the United States marshal she needed.

Yesterday she'd dodged reality. She'd spent the remainder of the day with him in the market. It was a place that provided little chance for serious talk. Later, she'd used Siobhan's presence to ward off any chance of him continuing to push her to go home. Now she wished that she could hit Rewind. The ploy had backfired especially in the evening when Siobhan had flirted shamelessly with him.

Tara had learned that even after all these years, she didn't like anyone else stepping between her and Trent.

When his intense blue eyes had locked with hers, she'd known that she was in trouble. She didn't trust herself alone with him. That was why she'd invited Siobhan to join them for a drink last night.

She needed a buffer against his seductive looks and strong will. And from his questions.

Tired after the emotional roller coaster of the day, she'd gone to bed early, shutting the door on the two of them and leaving them still chatting at a table in the courtyard.

This morning, the realization of all that had happened yesterday hit her full force. Now it was strange to think that Trent was sleeping on her couch in the tiny apartment that was too tight for two adults. The place had a hot plate and a fridge so small that it might be used in a camper. That, along with a quarter-size table was what defined one end of the room as the kitchen. The entire apartment was hardly more than one room with two closets. One closet for the bed and the second for the bathroom.

She stretched, yawned and stuck a toe out from under the blanket. She needed to sneak past him without waking him up. She wanted a few minutes to herself before the day began. Plus, she was craving a coffee that was a little more jazzed up than the one she could make in the apartment. She reserved that coffee for later in the day or evening. Now she thought she'd head down the street and pick up two coffees from a vendor, one for her and one for him. It would be kind of a peace offering for ignoring him much of yesterday.

She knew that she had to face him but first she wanted a few minutes alone and a start on her coffee. It was still early, shortly before seven o'clock. She got up and dressed. She opened the door and stepped out in her bare feet, her sandals in her hand with only a backward glance to the figure on her tiny sofa. Trent was sound asleep.

Outside, she passed vendors who were just setting up. Others had their wares out and called to her, urging her to give what they were selling a chance. Stray dogs and early shoppers added to the chaos.

Tara's attention was on her destination, a small cart at the bottom of the hill at the end of a long street. She'd discovered the stall yesterday. She'd been thrilled to find their coffee had a dark, rich nutty taste to it. It was too early in the morning to think of much other than her wake-up coffee.

TRENT WOKE UP with a start. Instinct told him that something had changed. And one thing he never did was ignore his instincts—they'd saved more than one life, including his own.

He sat up with his head pounding. His back ached from the rock-hard, too-small sofa. He hadn't planned to sleep. He was annoyed that he had. He'd been up late trolling the internet for information on one-half of the married couple who were her landlords. There'd been something about Carlos that had his instincts on high alert. He'd pretty much guessed that the man had worked in some sort of law enforcement capacity. That assumption hadn't been made because of anything that Carlos had said. Rather, it had been the assessing look he'd received on their brief introduction that had triggered a warning that there was something different about the man. There was a protective air to him that was different than a layman's stance. It had taken some work but he'd finally found a link that revealed that the man was different in a good way. He was a retired San Miguel de Allende police officer, and his last position, before retiring fifteen years ago, had been inspector.

He sat still for a moment thinking about what he'd learned, listening, gathering his senses. Light streamed through the window. A car horn sounded. In the apartment there was silence, as if he were alone in the place. He looked at his watch. It was just after seven o'clock in the morning.

"Tara! Are you in there?" he asked as he rapped on the bedroom door.

There was no sound. He didn't wait. He opened the door.

The room was empty.

He'd told her not to leave without him. He'd told her that it wasn't safe. But he'd forgotten the Tara he had known. Telling her not to do something would have been taken as a challenge. He'd seen hints yesterday that some things hadn't changed. He knew she continued to dance to her own drum, like she always had. Despite her fear, yesterday she'd stuck to her belief that San Miguel was safe. He'd found her because of a suggestion but social media had confirmed that clue. The bank robbers didn't know her at all. She was confident enough to listen to her own belief that she was safe here for now.

A rush of adrenaline ran through him. He couldn't

believe this was happening. But she hadn't left that long ago. He now realized that it was the click of the door as she closed it behind her that had awakened him.

His mind sped through the possibilities. For she'd never mentioned anything yesterday about leaving early, even though he'd spent the day shadowing her. She'd talked to shop owners and participated in a lesson on sidewalk painting. It had felt like he had, if not all the time in the world, at least enough to convince her that they needed to go back to the States.

It was only in the evening when things had seemed to change especially when they'd met her friend Siobhan for drinks. He couldn't get close to Tara with Siobhan there. So he'd endured Sioban's endless flirtations in an evening that seemed to drag on forever. The only bright spot had been Tara's reaction. She appeared to have lost her ability to smile. He wondered if she was jealous and couldn't help hoping she was. For him, there was still something there, something he felt for the girl who had broken his heart so many years ago.

Frustration seethed through him. Why couldn't she understand the danger she was in? He couldn't protect her if she wasn't here. He guessed that she'd gone to the market.

His gut screamed, "Danger."

He swore as he grabbed his shoes. He balanced on his left foot as he rammed a shoe on his right. The market was a place that she loved, and she could pick up breakfast or coffee there. Yesterday he'd learned more about her and her environment. Then, there'd been no immediate danger. Instead, he'd gotten to know more about her just by watching. He saw how she was quick to praise the work of the vendors and offer a smile. There had been no reason to believe that the danger level had changed. Now something was different. He sensed it and he knew that there was no time to question that feeling. He needed to find Tara.

The courtyard was empty.

In seconds, he was out the door and taking the stone steps to the main road in a series of leaps. He missed the last three steps as he hit the street.

He stopped in his tracks when his phone started ringing.

He yanked it out of his pocket and hit Talk as soon as he saw the number on the call display.

"Yeah, Jackson." He had nothing but respect for the man on the line. Still, a mother lode of impatience boiled through his veins. He didn't have time for this, but he couldn't ignore it; the call could be anything from a check-in to a complication that he needed to know about ASAP.

"I'm on a timer," he said shortly.

"Trouble," Jackson said and carried on before he could interrupt. "Another armed bank robbery. The good news is that we have an anonymous tip that gave us a name of a possible contact, Yago Cruz."

"Never heard of him."

"Unfortunately, I have. He belongs to a small cartel that's quickly becoming known." He listed a few other key members of the gang.

"Those names I know," Trent said. "The gang has been on the Mexican authorities' radar lately."

"There's a connection between them and Lucas Cruz. While Lucas is involved here with the gang that's been robbing banks, his brother, Yago, like I said, is a member of a Mexican cartel. Despite the small size of the cartel, they're involved in more crimes than you'd imagine—everything from drugs to murder. Worse, at least for us and this case, they have a solid network of connections. I'm afraid that if anyone can find her in Mexico, they can. If Lucas Cruz had anything to do with the break-in at the witness's house, then he knows that her flight took her to Mexico City and he's got the perfect man to greet her."

"If Lucas tries to chase her, he'd have to cross the border twice if he wanted to return back to the States," Trent said thoughtfully.

"The chance, with his background, that he'd make it across either way is remote."

"Unfortunately, engaging his brother is perfect. Lucas can have her chased down without ever leaving the States—" The words broke off as Trent clenched his fist and his heart seemed to speed up. Despite already speculating on that possibility, hearing it said aloud only reminded him of the danger Tara could face.

"Interestingly enough, the caller had details of a couple of robberies that only someone on the inside would know."

"So the caller wants to take Lucas Cruz down?"

"Probably. Whether this information is usable is my concern right now. So I did some research on Lucas Cruz. He'd been up on break-and-enters before and served time for petty theft and has no record of any recent employment in the last four years. It gets worse. There's evidence that Lucas Cruz and his brother have been in touch recently. What that connection was about we're not sure but—"

Trent interrupted Jackson with a curse. The implications of what he might be facing slammed into him. Despite that, he had a more immediate problem. His gut screamed at him that he needed to find Tara. There was no logical, no physical evidence—only instinct telling him to get moving. Right now, finding her superseded even this bit of intelligence. "Look, I've got a situation. I'm going to have to deal with this information later."

"Deal and call me back," Jackson said. "Immediately," he added in the split second before Trent disconnected.

He took a breath as he shoved the phone in his pocket. That was the beauty of Jackson. There was no need to explain the intricacies of working in the field. Not to him. Unlike others, Jackson had been there, put in his time. He knew both ends of the game—management and working in the field. That gave him the critical ability to assess any situation or at least sense when he needed to back off.

Trent wasn't downplaying Jackson's call. Cruz was important but finding Tara was crucial. That was his number one priority. He had to keep her safe, and to do that, he had to find her.

He couldn't guess what the contact might have been between Cruz and his brother. As Jackson had said, they could only assume the worst. Tara needed him. She needed protection.

He ran, veering around other pedestrians. He dodged vendors and their customers. He darted around a middle-aged man pushing a cart across the street. Some vendors were set up and others were still getting their wares in place. The street was a jumble of activity, moving toward organized chaos.

Where the hell was she?

For a moment, he second-guessed the gut feeling that had him here, chasing her down. But he couldn't, wouldn't dismiss the feeling that had rung true on too many assignments. The urgent sense that immediately followed the click of the door that had awakened him, hadn't lessened. It was a feeling that told him that this was the direction she was heading.

A dog barked. To his left, two children were jumping on and off the curb, laughing about everything and nothing as children do.

It felt as if time were the enemy. Jackson's call hadn't helped anything. A connection in Mexico was not good. She was the key to shutting down the gang's run of bank robberies. The stakes were high.

He scanned the street. It would have been so simple if he could have called. But she'd left anything trackable behind when she'd fled her home and country. He could see nothing but strangers. Locals and tourists but no Tara.

He clenched his teeth as a woman carrying an overflowing bag of vegetables jostled him. Her dark eyes met his and seemed full of silent apology as she pushed past him.

"Excuse me," he said as he bumped into a middle-aged man. Working his way into the middle of the street was like navigating an obstacle course. But in the center, should he ever get there, there were fewer people and he might be able to see something.

Jackson's call weighed on his mind. The fact that he'd easily found Tara also nagged at him. With the new information about Lucas Cruz's connections to Mexico, Trent realized that if it hadn't been difficult for him to find her, Cruz might find it equally easy.

I just know that I'm safe here.

He remembered Tara's insistence about that. He remembered her determination to cling to her independence. He hadn't rushed her to leave but he hadn't said that it was safe for her to be alone without him. It had been unspoken that danger was on the horizon, not that it had arrived. Now everything had changed. How close were Cruz's connections to finding her?

He'd had her social media history of San Miguel de Allende purged. But even the best computer teams couldn't remove everything. If the gang was good enough, they could have found her by trolling through her social media. They didn't need Enrique's mention of the city to know that if she'd been there once, she might well go there again.

She was an amateur at this. She needed to be home, under his protection, where he had full resources at his disposal. Here, it was just him and the possibility that the resources of an entire gang was being used to find her. Right now, for anyone with any skill, it was all too easy. She hadn't changed anything, not even the simplest thing, like her appearance or her name. It was something he'd meant to address today. Instead he found himself afraid that he might very well be behind the eight ball.

But this was all speculation. There was no proof that she was in danger. There were only his instincts. He kept moving, driven by the sense that something was terribly wrong.

Chapter Six

There's nothing better than a good cup of coffee in the morning.

Tara's voice echoed through Trent's mind like she was standing right there. She had told him that only yesterday. He cursed under his breath. He should have thought of that immediately. In one of the few moments when she'd seemed to let her guard down, she'd joked about the weak coffee served by her landlady. Then she'd pointed out the best coffee she'd found so far.

He picked up his pace, moving as fast as he could along the crowded street. He had no patience for delays. Jackson's words, the feel in the air, all of it was beyond troubling.

Yet, there was nothing tangible. Everything appeared normal.

He headed to where, only yesterday, she'd pointed out where the coffee vendor was. A group of children raced up one side, one stopped to ask for money and he gave the boy what change he had in his pocket.

"Gracias, senor," the boy said and ran past him, a half dozen other boys and a girl following close behind.

He tried to skirt a group of tourists. They all carried shopping bags with *San Miguel* stamped on them and clutched cameras as they clustered in the center of the street. He pushed past them and with little room to maneuver, jostled an elbow.

"Sorry," he threw over his shoulder. Still, a few choice words followed him.

His mind was already past them as he searched the crowd. But there was no sign of her. He only hoped that he was on a wild-goose chase and she was safely back at the apartment.

Then, a quarter of a block ahead, he knew he'd found trouble when he saw a tall dark-haired man with a mellow face that had an intense, focused look. But that wasn't the problem. It was what he held in his right hand. It was only a glimpse of dark metal that shone as the sun hit it. And then Trent's view was blocked as a woman moved into his line of sight. But he knew instinctively what the man held. He clenched his fists. He was too far away and there were too many people between them.

Trouble.

The man vanished into the crowd, and his path was blocked by a man pulling his cart across the street. He bit back frustration and veered right.

A woman screamed ahead of him. Tara or someone else, it didn't matter. What mattered was getting there and stopping the gunman before it was too late, before someone was hurt. If they weren't already.

"Damn it, where are you, Tara?" he muttered. Adrenaline raced through him. She had been so close and now she had slipped through his hands—again.

Then he saw her. Tara. A glimpse and then she was gone. But it was enough to know she was directly in a potential killer's path.

TARA HAD HOPED to have purchased her coffee and be well on her way home before the crowds hit the street. She hadn't factored in the approaching weekend nor those who'd begun arriving yesterday for next week's arts festival. Locals mixed with tourists, foreign transplants and the arts crowd.

The arts folk often came for long stays to study their art, whether it was painting or novel writing. San Miguel had it all. The market was a colorful mesh of people and things. Crafts and art combined with the tantalizing smells of the food trucks. She could visit this street every day and never get bored. That was a good thing, as she suspected she'd be here, or at least in Mexico, until it was safe back in Pueblo. Whether that was weeks, a month or two...

She thought of Trent. He didn't agree with any of that. In fact, he'd made it quite clear that that wasn't his agenda. He wanted her back in the States as soon as possible. That was something she refused to do until it was safe—on her terms, not his. For now, she was comfortable in the fact that she had convinced Trent to let her stay at least for the next few days.

But he'd made it clear that his presence was non-negotiable. He was here to the end.

She took a deep breath and focused on what had brought her here. The street sloped down a small hill, which would make it more of a challenge returning home. For now, it was a pleasant walk.

The breeze carried the scent of roasted coffee mixed with the smell of pastry and spices. Her stomach rumbled, reminding her that she hadn't had breakfast either.

Hopefully, she'd be back with the coffee before Trent woke up. It would be a peace offering or, more aptly, a tool to make sure he wasn't a hindrance in her life. Except he was already parked on her couch. She grimaced. He was a too-large presence in a too-small space. She wasn't sure how long she could act nonchalant about him being there, a few days even seemed forever. Her feelings for him were troubling and difficult to ignore. He'd always done that to her.

"Senorita!" a vendor called.

At another time she would have gone over to his stand, checked out the colorful blankets he was selling. But something told her to keep moving, so instead she simply nodded. She started to turn away when she was jostled and almost lost her balance. She swung around, backing away almost in the same move from the man who'd bumped her. She was sure that her face showed fear, unease, a myriad of emotions for the man she'd just bumped shoulders with looked at her oddly as he moved away.

She stepped backward, closer to the vendors.

She was farther from the open area in the street and closer to the fringes, where anything could happen and no one would see.

Trent.

Her unease was his fault with his talk of imminent danger and the need to protect her with a gun in hand. Now she was seeing trouble brewing everywhere.

He hadn't changed. He'd seen danger where there was none even in high school. He was forever drumming up the possibility of trouble. She would laugh and consider it a result of his love of spy and espionage movies. But even then, he'd had a sense when there was a problem, when things were about to implode. She imagined now, as a marshal, that instinct was much more honed. She didn't doubt what he told her yesterday, convinced by the sense of urgency with which he'd spoken. There was danger but she'd fled that danger. And no one could find her here.

Except, he'd found her.

Others could—just as he had said.

But she couldn't live in fear. She'd been proactive and that had brought her here. The fact that Trent was here, too, was something they'd deal with. They'd talk it out. He'd realize that she was thousands of miles from home, safe. He'd realize that she'd done the right thing.

Everything was the same as it had been before he arrived. The only thing that had changed was that she had a US marshal on her couch. And if she didn't hurry up and buy the coffee and get back, he would be on her tail.

But despite her best intentions, goose bumps prickled her skin and a chill ran through her. The feeling of unease stuck with her. She looked over her shoulder. And that was when her worst nightmare came true.

A gleam of black metal glinting in the sun. The stare of a man who stood above the others. Even from this distance, she knew that once again she was looking at the wrong end of a gun. She did the only thing she could.

She ran.

Chapter Seven

Trent swore and broke into a run.

Tara.

She was his only thought, his only motivation. He was here to protect her. He'd give his life for her. The thoughts blazed through his mind without a filter, without will. They were just there, the motivation for everything he did now.

His right hand went to his side. Of course, the gun wasn't there. He felt its absence more than at any other time, for now he needed it. He was a no-carry here in Mexico. Here, he was armed only with his skill at hand-to-hand combat. He was an expert at it, having perfected the art over the years.

But hand-to-hand combat did not bridge the space between him and the potential threat, and it didn't fire warning shots. Still, he knew that his expertise was another reason that Jackson hadn't turned him down for this assignment. As long as he had his wits and his hands—he was never unarmed.

He dodged a couple and pushed a cart aside. A motor scooter was being walked through the congested street. The owner was one step from getting in his way. Trent pushed past him. Someone cursed him out in Spanish.

He didn't care. Nothing mattered but keeping Tara safe. Nothing mattered except stopping the potential for carnage ahead, to protect Tara.

A gunshot cracked through the crowd, spinning it into chaos. Someone screamed. Another scream joined the first, and then the crowd broke into a churn of panicked people moving in every direction.

A man with a gun in this crowd—the reality had Trent's insides turning to ice. He couldn't think of the possibilities of that reality, of the fact that Tara might be hurt along with so many others.

Tara.

He was moving as fast as he could, looking in every direction for a glimpse of her blond hair. Finally, he broke through into a less crowded area with a better view down the street. A quarter of a block ahead, he caught a glimpse of the gunman but not Tara. He pushed forward but was blocked by a woman with two small children. They were moving toward the gunman.

"Go back," he said in Spanish, schooling his voice to reflect nothing but calm and control. "There's a man with a gun ahead."

More chaos erupted as others nearby heard his words. But there was no avoiding that—the mention of a gun was inflammatory but necessary.

Trent moved away from it all, breaking into a jog, slowing to dodge another person. He found himself blocked by a vendor and a slim young man who was moving in the same direction but not fast enough.

He grabbed the man's arm and pulled him back and out of his way.

The young man turned on him, his fists clenched, his dark eyes flashing.

"Let go, you—"

The expletive was lost on Trent. Instead, Trent had him on the ground in one twist. He stepped around him, the expletives only meaningless echoes.

"Go back," he repeated his warning. "There's a man firing a gun ahead."

He needed to lay eyes on Tara. He needed to know she was all right. Only one night and a day into his assignment, and he was already coming up with dismal odds.

He couldn't and wouldn't allow this to continue. She would live because anything else would mean failure—he wouldn't have it.

And then he saw her and for a moment everything stopped. She was right in the path of the gunman.

TARA'S HEART POUNDED. She wanted to believe that it was her imagination, that the glint of dark metal meant nothing. But she knew what it was. She'd seen guns before, many times. She was familiar with makes and models, which ones were good for skeet, which for hunting ducks, which for defense. She'd heard her grandfather talk of them and seen them often at his house. He'd been a gun enthusiast. As a kid, she'd been enthralled by his vast collection.

But it was guns that had taken her grandfather from her, and after that, her father. Her grandfather had died in a senseless accident at the hands of his neighbor. They'd been hunting and the neighbor claimed to have mistaken a movement in the woods for game. Instead, he'd shot her grandfather. The neighbor had been charged and despite his intentions, he had spent some time in jail. None of that brought her grandfather back. As an adult, she was no fan of firearms. She'd learned the hard way that a weapon used to defend could also be used to kill. And then there was the recent bank robbery. Now Tara felt even more that guns were merely instruments of death.

"Get ahold of yourself," she muttered. She had to focus on what was going on now. She knew she needed to lead the gunman away, keep others safe. Hopefully she could do it without getting shot herself.

Her heart beat wildly. How had he found her? And who was he?

What was certain was that he was following her. She knew that others might not have noticed him—despite his height, the number of other shoppers made it easy for him to blend in. But she'd been trained long ago, as a child, to keep an eye open for anything unusual. It was a skill she'd always be grateful to her grandfather for.

She feared that he would break out of the crowd

and they'd be face-to-face. If that happened, she would have nowhere to go, nowhere to hide.

"Breathe," she muttered to herself. She had to clear her mind of the muck of panicked thoughts. She needed to get out of here, make herself safe and do it without endangering anyone else. As she took a breath and tried to make sense of it all, she saw him again. The gun was aimed straight at her. There was no doubting his intent now.

"Run!" she screamed at the crowd. She would save every one of them if she could.

People pushed around her. A bag of groceries dropped. Vegetables lay strewed around them. The crowd was too tight and her voice was not enough. The gunman was again swallowed up in the swirl of people. Her life was in danger, but her presence was threatening the lives of so many others. She had to get out of here, for herself, for them. Her heart pounded as she thought of the dangers of a panicked crowd, the deadly intent of a handgun…

A shot came so close that she could almost feel the heat. A woman screamed but the sound was swallowed in the chaos.

This was no coincidence. Trent's warning ran through her mind. He'd been right. It was clear that she hadn't run far enough.

There wasn't time to think of what she should have done. She had to deal with now. Lead the danger away from a place where too many people could get hurt. She thought that she might faint. Her heart was like a drum that had gone mad in her chest. She wasn't sure if she wasn't having a heart attack. She veered right and away from the crowd.

And then she was tackled from behind and slammed to the ground—and she knew that it was over.

Chapter Eight

Trent cursed the Fates. The shooter should never have gotten as close to Tara as he had. Trent might have gravely injured her tackling her like that. He hadn't been able to control much of the fall. He'd taken her down with his whole weight. But it had been his only option to save her life.

Now Tara lay still, her face to the ground. Was she dead? Injured?

His heart pounded so hard he could feel it. A bitter taste ran through his mouth. He couldn't even think of what he wanted to do to the piece of slime who was hunting her down. He raised up on an elbow, lifting some of his weight from her. This was completely on him. Regret and frustration raced through him. His hand again reached for his absent weapon. He should have somehow intervened sooner. That had been impossible, he knew that.

"Tara, are you all right?" He couldn't keep the desperate edge from his voice. She needed to be okay. He couldn't consider the other option.

He'd managed to miss having her head crack on

the cobbles, but she hadn't moved in the few seconds since. It had been a tricky maneuver. He'd flipped his own body and taken the brunt of the fall, spinning twice. He'd done his best to use his body to shield hers.

"Trent? I can't breathe."

"Are you hurt, sweetheart?" he asked as he rolled off her.

He sat up, looking for danger, for the shooter. There was no sign of him. He turned to Tara. "Are you hurt?" he repeated.

"No, I—" Her voice broke off as tears welled and slipped down her cheek. She wiped them with the back of her hand. "I'm fine. Overwhelmed—relieved," she added.

"Hang on," he said. He stood and scanned the street looking for any sign of danger, searching for the shooter. But he was gone, vanished into the crowd. He'd disappeared as quickly as he'd appeared. Around them, people milled, looking confused, almost unsure of what had happened.

Trent reached for her hand and pulled her to her feet. "I want you to stay here," he said.

She didn't say anything. The silence wasn't like her. But nothing now was as it should be, nothing was the norm. It was clear she was in shock. He led her over to an abandoned vendor's cart that held a collection of sports and sun hats. "Sit there and wait for me, please."

She nodded, as if words were more than she could bear.

"Don't move and stay behind the cart where you can't be seen."

Their eyes met. Hers were dark and glazed with fear. He'd do anything to take that fear away.

"I'll be right back," he said to her.

"It's too dangerous, Trent. Wait for the authorities to come to us."

He wasn't sure if she realized what she'd said or what his role was here. It was as if she'd excluded him from the circle he belonged to. Even here in Mexico, he was still part of that general term, *the authorities*. Visiting, but nonetheless an authority.

"Stay down," he said.

"Trent—"

"Trust me," he interrupted. "You'll be safe. I won't be gone long."

Before she could argue the point further, he moved into the street. He kept to the outside, where he could find cover by vendors' carts. But there was nothing to take cover from.

Sirens sounded in the distance. The gunman had disappeared. A cluster of a mix of local shoppers and tourists huddled in an alcove. Another group gathered around a vendor's cart. A few carts stood abandoned. Ahead, the street was more crowded— the panic seemed to have kept to the immediate area.

Trent was back in the middle of the road, trying to get a handle on the situation. There were a number of vendors up ahead who were gathering up goods that had fallen to the ground. An elderly couple lurked on the edge of the sidewalk, taking shelter behind an umbrella. He could feel their eyes on him as if he were the threat. Many others had headed uphill away from the chaos, where he and Tara had come from. Two hundred feet in the opposite direction, the street ran downhill toward an intersection. He knew that was where the emergency workers and police would enter the area. It was the easiest and quickest approach and from the sounds of the sirens, their arrival was imminent.

He caught sight of a dark head, taller than average. It was him, the man with the gun, and he was half a block ahead. But even that seemed more distant than it was with the amount of people still on the street. The man was moving fast as if attempting to escape.

"Crap," Trent muttered. He broke into a jog. He dodged clusters of confused and frightened shoppers, moving as fast as he could downhill.

Then he saw the sleek nut-brown SUV at the next intersection. He broke into a run. Tension made his jaw ache, and his fists clenched. The slime had a way out. He shoved a man aside and pulled a woman out of his way. But he was too late. He saw the back end of the vehicle as it turned a corner and made its escape.

There were no words to describe his frustration. He used a few foul options, but they didn't do anything to make the situation any better. The distance between them was troubling. He couldn't run that fast. And more than likely, even if he could—the occupants of that vehicle were all armed and they'd fire back. It wasn't just his life to be concerned about.

There were shoppers still lingering in clusters, vendors trying to protect their wares. People without the sense to take cover.

He blew out a frustrated breath. If he could, he'd give it his all to end this piece of crap's career. But he had neither the tools nor the opportunity. The man was going to get away.

He'd been unable to get a visual on the driver or any of the other occupants. What he knew was that there were three people in that vehicle. And that told him nothing.

He swore again. The sirens were no longer wailing in the distance but sounded as if they were seconds away. Things were heating up, and US marshal or not, he was a foreigner. There'd be questions, and he couldn't afford to be detained by the local authorities. He needed to get a plan in action and make sure Tara was safe. She needed to be in the States, where he had the resources to protect her. There could be no further delays.

As he jogged back to her, he called Enrique. He needed his help to smooth the way with the local authorities. As a foreigner, caught in the middle of a shootout in a city that wasn't known for violent crime, he might be highly suspect.

"Enrique," he said. "I've got a situation. A shooter in the market." He gave him the details of what had happened.

"I'll contact the San Miguel police and make sure you're not detained for any reason," Enrique promised. "A standard interview, you're not going to get away from that. But I'll make sure I'm there when it's happening, conference call. Hour tops. You have my word on it."

Trent ended the call and headed back to where he'd left Tara.

She was gone.

He asked the vendor in Spanish where the blond-haired American woman had gone. As much as he'd hated the fact that she hadn't changed her hair color or length, he was glad for it now. He would be able to easily find her. But the vendor admitted to only see-ing her briefly and having no idea where she went.

Trent retraced his steps and then stopped. Ahead, he saw a small crowd focused on something in its center. What the hell was going on? His heart skipped as he thought that someone might be hurt.

Tara.

"I'm a doctor," a male voice said at his right elbow. A man moved past him after making that pronounce-ment.

Those words had Trent bursting into a jog, and he followed the husky gray-haired man, who pushed his way through the crowd.

Tara.

Where was she?

And then he was through and could see a woman on the ground. But it wasn't Tara.

Instead, Tara was at the woman's side. She was pulling a blanket, obviously borrowed from a nearby vendor, over her. Relief flooded through him as he remembered her penchant for helping people. She was always the Good Samaritan. But damn it, he thought, she didn't need to be that here. Not when that could mean life or death. Especially as she didn't know that the gunman had left, that the danger was over. She'd known none of that and still she'd insisted on potentially risking her life to help someone else.

She looked up and her eyes locked with his.

He crouched down beside her. "You weren't there where I left you. You scared the hell out of me," he said as he quickly surveyed the woman lying in front of them. "Shot?"

Tara nodded. "She's conscious."

"That's good news," he said as the doctor moved past him. "That and you're safe." He knew there was an angry edge to his voice. But he'd been scared that somehow, despite the fact that the gunman was gone, she'd been hurt.

"I'm sorry," she said. "I saw a commotion here and realized someone needed help." She shook her head. "Are you all right?"

He nodded. "Whoever he was, he's gone, if that's what you're asking. It's over."

"Because of you. You scared him off," she said softly.

He shook his head. He'd done no such thing.

She looked at him in a way that seemed to reach into his soul, into the very essence of him. It was a look that had brought his younger self many times to his knees.

"You saved my life," she said. "There are no words to thank you for that, Trent. But words are all I have. Thank you." She looked at the woman. "You may have saved hers, too, and a lot of others."

"I did nothing," Trent said. Except let a gunman escape, he thought. Damn it. Frustration rolled through him.

Tara shook her head. "You hunted the shooter down. He ran because of you. And this lady will hopefully live. That's all on you. There would have been more shots fired if you hadn't intervened." The last words shook slightly, as if she were just becoming fully aware of all that had happened. "More people injured or even dead."

"I should have caught him."

"How?" she asked with that practical edge that had driven him crazy as a teenager. "There were too many people. Too many potential casualties."

She was right. This wasn't the Tara of his youth. She'd matured into someone he desperately wanted to get to know.

Her eyes burned with passion, but she trembled as if her legs wouldn't hold her. He put his hands on her shoulders, to steady her.

"The crowd was against you," she said as she leaned into him. "You did everything you could."

The doctor stood up.

"I don't think the bullet hit any major organs," he said. The slight accent was the only indication that English was not his first language. "We'll get her to the hospital and she'll be fine."

"I can't believe this happened. Without you, Trent…" Tara's voice trailed off.

But they both knew where her unfinished sentence would have gone. The gunman had been after her. He wanted her dead, and without Trent, that was what would have happened.

"It's over," he said, hoping to calm her. "He's gone."

"I thought it was safe here. I thought I had gone far enough and instead I've brought danger with me to San Miguel."

She folded her arms across her chest. "I caused this. If I hadn't been here…" she whispered. "I tried to lead him out of the market. And at least one person got shot as a result." Her voice broke. "This is my fault."

"This wasn't on you."

"If not me, who?"

He knew exactly who the target had been, who it would always be. She couldn't outrun it. But it wasn't her fault. She needed to be with him so that he could keep her safe. He met the trepidation in her brown eyes and took her arm. "Let's get through this, then we'll talk."

She was silent and despite everything that had happened, she seemed calm, poised even. There were no tears. He couldn't believe how calm she was. She was a civilian, an artist, unused to such things. And here she was comforting others, shouldering the blame where she had no fault.

"You saved people by running and leading him away," he said. "Don't ever forget that."

He took her in his arms and without thinking, he

kissed her. It was a mistake from the beginning and there was no going back. Her lips were generous and rich beneath his.

"Trent, no," she said and then gently pushed him back. "This isn't the time or place."

"You're right," he said. He wasn't sure what he'd been thinking. Or really, not thinking at all. Just feeling her presence—relieved that she was alive, remembering what they'd been. He wasn't sentimental and yet all of that was sentimental nonsense. It was hardly enough to call it the *wrong time and place*. He'd been out of line on both the job front and the relationship front. But she did that to him.

She looked up at him and put a hand on his shoulder. The touch burst through his thoughts but it was her words that had the final impact.

"Never may be the time or place. I think we outgrew that part of our relationship a long time ago."

"Of course. That's over," he said. But something died inside him at her words. In his heart, he hoped that wasn't how she really felt. He hoped that, right now, she was just frightened. Because, he was falling for her again, or if he was honest with himself, he'd never gotten over her at all.

Chapter Nine

"The first responders are here," Trent said. It was an unnecessary announcement. But he felt like he needed to say something. As he'd guessed, they were leaving their vehicles at the intersection. "I'm going to go down to meet them. You'll be okay?" He spoke as if nothing had come before, as if she hadn't told him that for her, any relationship they could have had was over. Right now, none of that mattered. He'd heard worse in his lifetime.

"Trent, I'm sorry for getting you into this. I don't care what you—"

"No." He put a hand on her arm. She didn't have to say the words. He knew what they were. "Don't say it. We'll talk later. Stay here. I'm going to talk to the police."

"Are you sure? Should I go with you? I—"

"No, not now. Wait here. Please."

She nodded. "I will. I promise."

He had to trust that this time she'd put her safety first. He needed to touch base with the police. He needed to make sure that his mission was not hampered by his position as a foreigner. He was counting on Enrique but the personal touch might help.

He headed down the street to the intersection where the emergency vehicles were beginning to congregate. He hoped that Enrique had put everything in place and there would be no red tape to wade through. He didn't need any delays. He had to bring Tara home as quickly as possible.

If things went smoothly, they could be on a flight as soon as tonight. He was sure that, after this, Tara would have no objections to going home. He hoped today had proved to her that Mexico was no longer the safe place she'd imagined. The gang had found her.

The truth was that he feared they could find her anywhere in Mexico. They had connections; Jackson had already confirmed that. Except they knew little about this cartel, only an awareness of a few of the leaders and little about the man who was a brother to one of the bank robbers. That placed Trent at a disadvantage. What he didn't know only fueled the urgency. He hoped Jackson could tell him more. One misstep here, and something like today could happen again, only she could die. Someone else might die.

She didn't have the resources to disappear on her own. She needed him. If anyone could keep her safe, he could. It wasn't arrogance that had him thinking that. He knew his limitations and he knew what he was good at. He was good at disappearing. He'd done it many times in his career, both for himself and for others.

Around him, people milled about, waiting for what would happen next. It was like the main show had hit intermission. With the panic gone, they looked more interested than upset. Some of them were even smiling and others watched curiously.

Emergency vehicles with sirens and flashing lights had become the show. A police car had parked three hundred yards down the street at the intersection. Another inched its way up the street and then backed up, stopping in exactly the same spot where the shooter had so recently escaped.

Trent kept going, dodging pockets of former shoppers and street vendors. This was the troubling part of any investigation, any disaster—the propensity for curiosity to overpower common sense. People were getting in the way of emergency crews. And like most crowds, they not only completely failed to help but instead hindered the investigative process.

The paramedics were moving up the street with a stretcher. It was easier coming in on foot and more than likely faster than trying to navigate the crowd and the narrow street in the ambulance. In the two minutes it took Trent to weave his way to the intersection, it was now crawling with emergency vehicles.

Doors slammed, lights splashed across the cobblestones. He scanned the crowd, his gaze finally locking onto the one man who appeared to be in charge. He was short and wiry but was bellowing orders as he stood in a way that commanded respect.

As Trent headed toward the man, more sirens

wailed in the distance. A police car took the last available space in the junction where the two roads met. Six police officers were moving up the street. They had their guns in hand as they cleared a path for the paramedics bringing another stretcher up the steep incline. The cobbled street and the slope, along with the people milling around, didn't make any of it an easy feat.

"Trent Nielsen," he said to the man he believed to be in charge, holding out his hand as he approached. "US marshal."

"Jorge Peraz," the officer said. He frowned as he looked at Trent, as if he didn't quite trust him. "I spoke to Enrique. He vouched for you." His tone suggested that without that, he would have gladly detained him. "United States marshal," he repeated. "I hope you don't expect special treatment."

"That's not what this is about," Trent replied. It wasn't anything the man had said, being as he'd said little. Still, he disliked Jorge Peraz and his attitude.

"If this is about your authority here, I'm not disputing that. My only concern is what's happened."

"Fair enough," Trent said, surprised and a little disconcerted.

"Okay, what have you got?"

"A visual on the gunman. Dark hair, tall, maybe six feet, with a light brown complexion."

"Mexican?"

"I've no evidence to say one way or another. What I do know is that he seemed to be acting alone," Trent said. "But he was picked up well over five minutes ago there." He pointed. "By a brown Ford SUV. Besides the shooter, there was a driver and a passenger. I didn't get a close look at either, but both looked to be males. The driver was wearing a navy ball cap. But I couldn't get much else. The street was pretty congested then. But it appeared to be a planned pickup."

Trent's jaw tightened. A planned pickup was the logical way to go, anyone in law enforcement knew that. In a situation like this, the shooter needed to either martyr himself or have a planned exit. Martyr wasn't the cartel's way.

He pushed the thoughts away and focused on Jorge. He had to remind himself not to react to anything the man might say. Instead, he allowed him to take the lead. If he spoke up, stepped on the man's pride, he'd only get more resistance.

Jorge's dark eyes were fixed on Trent as if he would be able to ferret out a lie just by staring at him. "I suppose you also know who's responsible?"

"Of course not." Trent couldn't contain his frustration. He also wasn't giving Jorge everything he did know. That the shooter was after Tara. "I'm saying that I saw the shooter leave the area. There was only one."

"You're saying a lot." The man's voice had an edge. "We'll need you down at the station to get your report."

What was he about? Trent thought. Was the officer threatening him? The way Jorge was reacting wasn't quite what Trent had anticipated. He hadn't been able to get a complete read on the man but what he'd seen so far, he didn't like. And he didn't trust him.

He gave the officer a brief nod, reminding himself that he was a foreigner. This was not his country and that made Peraz the authority. They both knew it.

"Police headquarters in an hour. I'll see you there," Jorge said. He took down Trent's name and number before moving up the street to catch up with his men.

Trent stood, thinking that so far what he had seen was a piss-poor way to run any police operation. He could take off and they'd never see him again, he realized. He was left standing alone at the fringes of the street where he'd left Tara.

Tara. He needed to get back to her.

As he headed up the street, he remembered that he also needed to call Jackson back. In all that had happened, he'd forgotten to find out what Jackson had left unsaid. That wasn't good. His mind usually hopped from one task to the next, forgetting none as others lined up. The fact that this had been a chaotic emergency shouldn't have changed that. But he knew in his heart what had changed it: Tara.

He felt things for her that he never thought he would. All these years later, he was a different person, as was she. And yet, in some ways, although they'd grown up, nothing had changed at all. At least not for him.

He thought how lucky they'd been, all of them. There was one known casualty when there could have been so many more. And she was going to be okay. Worse, there could have been fatalities.

He glanced around. The crowd was starting to thin. He wondered if the police had interviewed any of them.

He strode to the side of the street, out of the main flow of traffic. He was heading back to where he had left Tara, trying to stay out of the way. At the same time, he had his phone out and was making a call.

"What's going on?" Jackson asked the moment he answered.

He explained the last twenty minutes in terse words. The explanation was condensed into seconds. He was still moving forward, his long stride eating up the distance between him and Tara. "What else do you have, Jack?"

"A recent robbery in Albuquerque that we're sure is connected to the one Tara witnessed. One of the bank clerks heard one of the robbers speaking in Spanish. She's Mexican herself and she linked the accent to Mexico. Unfortunately she couldn't pin any one state. She said she didn't hear him clearly enough to tag anything but a country. We've got an alert at the border crossing."

"The circle of trust, Trent, isn't always as wide as you'd like to make it. Watch it, that's all I've got to say. The authorities don't always have your back. I've no specifics or I'd obviously tell you. Just keep your eyes open. This has gotten stickier than I'd like. And I want you home with the witness, pronto."

Jackson disconnected soon after that. Trent had been walking all the while he was talking. Now he looked up to discover that he was almost at the peak of the street and at the exact spot where he'd left Tara. He glanced across the street through the remaining onlookers and the emergency personnel to see Tara heading toward him. There was a relieved look on her face and behind him was the scowling face of Jorge.

He ignored the police officer and met Tara in two strides. He took her by the shoulders.

"I'm fine, Trent," she said before he could ask. She smiled, but her smile was shakier than it was steady. "Nothing has changed except that they've got the gunshot victim stabilized and almost ready to transport."

Despite her words, there was a look of concern as well as relief on her face. Tara's face had always been open. What she felt showed in her eyes, in her expression. Regardless of her earlier rejection and the words that had drawn blood, she reached tentatively for his hand. He closed his hand over hers, feeling the warm pulse of her palm against his. It had been a long time since he'd held her hand. It was a memory that came back with a rush of nostalgia.

"I don't like this, Trent," she whispered. "I don't trust him." She glanced back at Jorge. "It's like he thinks I'm at fault or something."

Circle of trust.

Jackson's phrase came back to haunt him. Where was Trent in the trust factor? A foreigner, a US marshal in the midst of a violent event in what was only yesterday a quiet market area in the heart of the city. His guard was up. He wasn't quite sure who he could trust. He only knew what he was sworn to do, protect Tara above all else.

At the police station, the process was efficient if dry. There was a "let's get it over with" attitude. He found that strange but no different than the initial talk with Jorge. He guessed it was because of Enrique's intervention.

The police had taken Tara's statement. But their questions soon dried up when they discovered that she was unable to give a description of the suspect. Unfortunately, she'd only had a glimpse of a gun, the dark hair and an estimated height, and nothing else except how many shots were fired. There were a dozen people in the area who could tell them the same and they'd interviewed them at the scene.

"I'll meet you at my place," she said to him after she'd been told that the police had no further questions for her.

"No. Stay here with me."

"Senor. Let the lady go. We—"

"No, you don't understand," he interrupted. And then stopped, realizing that there was only so much he could reveal.

"It's all right," Tara insisted.

"There is no need for the lady to wait," the police officer said.

And it was clear the police officer was getting impatient.

He liked none of this. He wanted to tell the police where they could take their statement. "She should stay with me, considering everything that's happened," he said, making one last attempt.

"Senor, the lady is done here. She'll be fine. A taxi is waiting."

He took both her hands. "Go straight home."

"I will," she said.

Her face was pale but there was a calm thread in her words.

With no choice, he finally gave in. He had to wait for Jorge, who wanted to do a final interview. He was getting different treatment because of his status as a marshal. Unfortunately, as a witness, there wasn't anything more that he could add.

He watched as she walked out. Her stride, despite everything that had happened, had a sureness about it. She was different than the girl he remembered. The physical change was obvious; her curves had been sweet but now they were the seductive lines of a woman. Even her manner was much more self-assured. He supposed she could say the same about him. How he was different from the boy she remembered.

Jorge entered the room a few minutes later. He glanced at the empty seat where Tara had been and shrugged. "We've got more than I anticipated. An eyewitness who managed to take a picture. I just wanted you to get a look at what you might be up against."

He had a tablet in one hand. He stood at the other side of the desk, looking at it. Then he handed it to Trent. "Here it is. Take a look."

The picture was a bit blurry. The subject had been in motion. It didn't tell Trent much that he didn't already know. It did allow him to identify the weapon. A handgun. A Glock, to be specific. But what was more disturbing was the angle of the gun and the juxtaposition of the people in the picture. He could see that the gun had been aimed where Tara had stood. A shudder ran through him and he was flooded by relief at the fact that she'd come out unscathed. He was also relieved that she wasn't here to see this and be reminded at how close she'd come to being hurt. Or worse.

"I'd know that SOB anywhere," Jorge said. He flipped to another screen that showed a string of wanted pictures. "Yago Cruz. He belongs to a cartel that has been nothing but a pain in the butt. Fortunately, I had nothing to do with them until now. They were a low-level cartel until they made their presence known here in Guanajuato State." He shook his head. "I'd heard rumors a few years ago but to have them here..." He slammed his fist on the desk.

Trent thought that in an odd way the reaction was almost overdramatic, as if instead of being upset Jorge might be just the opposite. It was only an

odd hunch and it did nothing to change his circumstances. He let the thought blow by.

Instead, Jackson's words ran through his mind
and he wondered again what they meant or if they
meant anything at all in this context.

Circle of trust.

Chapter Ten

*Never may be the time or place. I think we outgrew
that part of our relationship a long time ago.*

Tara would never forget saying those words or
forgive herself for the insensitive way in which she'd
said them. Worse, she hadn't meant any of it. Not
like that, not like they'd come out. The truth that lay
in those words wasn't in the hurtful parts. Instead,
that had been the terrified part of her speaking. She
treasured the memories of their earlier relationship.
She always had.

But having Trent here, the first sight of him, had
brought back feelings she wasn't comfortable with.
It was why she'd used Siobhan as a buffer yesterday,
but now everything had changed. Trent had amazed
her with his ability to jump in, to protect her and
others. Not only that, but he was probably wrap-
ping up the whole incident in a concise presentation
to the authorities. Or at least that was what she assumed; he'd been gone just over an hour. He'd been
a boy she'd admired and now he was the man who
was threatening to claim her heart.

Tara pushed the thoughts from her mind. Rather than returning to her apartment as she'd promised, she was waiting for Trent at a small outdoor café at the top of the hill. It was safe. The crisis was over. And she was only a quarter of a block away from her apartment. She felt comfortable here with the sun beating down and a Spanish classic playing over the speakers. It was like this morning had never happened. This was an oasis in the middle of the chaos. It was a place where she could gather her thoughts.

And, truthfully, she didn't want to face her landlords. She knew that they would have questions, especially knowing that she'd been in the market. For, as she'd been leaving this morning, Francesca had stopped for a few words before heading inside to make breakfast. Considering what had happened, and knowing that she had been there, it was only natural that there'd be questions. She'd prefer to have Trent at her side to present a united story. Would he tell them the truth? She wasn't sure if she even knew what was real and what was fiction, what needed to be said and what didn't.

How did they explain their involvement? Lies might be simple but their telling became complex. And the truth—what, exactly, was that? Something she hardly knew herself. Her location had become a secret until the trial was over. How long that would be, she didn't know. Since the moment she'd fled that bank, everything had changed. Now it seemed that she was a danger to both herself and others.

She took a sip of the virgin margarita she'd ordered

while she waited for Trent, and wished she'd ordered something stronger. She set the glass down and pulled a notepad from her bag. She began sketching with the pencil that was never not with her. It was calming. But art always was, even this project, which was overdue.

She hadn't wanted to draw the gunman. His face had haunted her since the robbery. But she was here because of what she'd seen. It was time to share what the bank robber had looked like. It was time to sketch what she remembered. It would be needed.

A taxi drove by and stopped at the top of the hill at the base of the steps that led to her rental.

"Trent!" Tara called, waving her arms.

She knew the minute he spotted her, the minute she saw his frown as he approached, that he wasn't pleased she hadn't gone home.

"Why didn't you go back?" Trent asked. "This isn't safe."

"It is safe, Trent. This whole area. You made it that way." She looked up from the face she'd been drawing. It was the man from the bank robbery in Pueblo. She'd lightly penciled the lines of his cheekbones. She'd added the fire to his dark eyes that had been both troubled and terrifying. The man haunted her and it had been tough bringing that memory to life in her art. Despite that, she'd sketched him from every angle she could remember. And now, with Trent's eyes watching her, she continued to sketch.

"That's him? The bank robber?" he asked. He watched her shade in here, add a bit more dimension there.

She nodded. "I'll draw something better at home, where I have a drawing pencil and sketchbook. But I couldn't wait. I didn't think I should wait any longer."

"Can I?" he asked as he reached for the small pad.

"Sure, go ahead."

He frowned as he analyzed the various angles of the face she'd sketched. "This is amazing," he said. "From these sketches, I'd easily recognize him on the street. We don't need anything more than this unless there's a detail you missed."

"Thanks," she said. "Hopefully it does the job and you catch him."

He took pictures of her sketches and then texted them to someone.

"What did the police want from you?" she asked. "What did they ask?"

"Everything I could tell them about the connection to the robbery in the States."

"And you think they'll be of any help? And how did you know what not to tell them?" It was hard to decide in Mexico which police one could trust and which they couldn't. She wondered how he'd known what to reveal or if the person he was speaking to was trustworthy. After all, he was here because of a foreign country's criminal issue.

"I have a contact with the federal police. We wasted close to an hour in a back-and-forth with Enrique's office in Mexico City. But the police are satisfied we've told them everything they need."

"So, what do we do now?" She met his eyes, which seemed afire with determination.

"I can protect you more easily in the States. But we've been through that. I know you didn't agree but I think now the choice is clear. We need to go back. You know that, don't you?"

Something in her froze. The last thing she wanted to do was go home. But she knew now that she wasn't safe in Mexico either, or at least not in San Miguel de Allende. She looked into Trent's stormy blue eyes and remembered all they'd once had. She wondered what his life had been like in the time since. She assumed by his actions that he was single now. But that didn't mean he didn't have children or ex-wives or ex-girlfriends. She almost smiled at the plural, but Trent was a good-looking man.

"I need to get you home, where I can make sure you're safe," he said breaking into her thoughts and forcing her back to a disturbing reality. "We can't waste any time getting you into witness protection."

A shiver ran through Tara at the thought of going back and of what he was asking of her. She didn't want to say it and yet right now, it was the elephant in the room. It was the fear that held her back, that kept her from saying yes, that made her want to run. He deserved to know.

"Tara?"

Seconds seemed to tick by as slowly as minutes before she could form the words. "My dad was in witness protection. He believed the authorities could protect him."

He put his hands over hers as if he knew where this was going. And he well might. Her dad's plight had been no secret, not to the authorities who had arranged witness protection. She looked in his eyes and saw the truth. He knew but it didn't matter. This was about her, about her facing her worst nightmare. This had to be said.

"He believed them, believed the cops and their promises of safety." Her voice shook, the words choked in her throat.

"You're not your dad."

"I tell myself that. It hasn't helped." She shrugged but the tears were threatening as they always did when she spoke of this, or even thought of it. That was why she never did, at least in recent years. There was nothing easy about this; no matter how hard she tried to put it in the past, it seemed determined to be part of her present.

"It doesn't change anything. It doesn't change the fact that he was killed while walking across a street in a strange town. It doesn't change the fact that he died with his family miles away or that police protection failed in the worst way possible."

"I'm sorry, Tara. I wish I could change what happened. I wished at the time, too."

"You knew back then? How?" That was a surprise, she thought. He'd still been a kid, like her.

"Only by rumors after I..." He stopped and cleared his throat. "Suffice it to say, I heard."

"You looked me up," she said with disbelief in her voice.

"It must be tough," he said as he skated over her

accusation. "I couldn't imagine losing my mom. Her house is the family gathering place.".

She knew that his dad had died in a traffic accident when he was very young. As a teenager, he'd said regretfully that he couldn't remember him. And that he couldn't miss the man he'd never known. For her, it was different.

"Sometimes it's like I just lost him."

"And you don't trust authorities because of it," he finished. "Because of your father."

She nodded and wiped her eyes with the back of her hands.

"I was fifteen," she said, as if stating the details, as if retelling the event would somehow give her the strength to do what she knew needed to be done. She couldn't hide here any longer but the alternative terrified her. "Just after I left Pueblo."

"I heard the full details many years later. But I've always wanted to reach out. I thought of you—of the pain you went through—often."

She couldn't help herself; her hands trembled but her gaze caught and held his. The empathy, the strength she saw there almost prompted her to say yes to his demands. Yet she couldn't. Like she'd told him, she'd seen firsthand what could happen if she were to stay here. She had to make her excuses and get out. But she couldn't leave with him either. She wouldn't endanger him. What had happened in the market only confirmed everything he had said. She wouldn't endanger anyone else. They were after her and as long as he wasn't with her, he'd be safe. There was only one way to accomplish that. She needed to leave here without him. Except he would refuse to allow it if he knew. She was the reason he was here.

She would have to trick him. Go with the flow and take him by surprise because there was no way she could get around him and just take off. Trent was too smart for that; he always had been.

He held her hands tighter and his gaze never left hers.

"That was the past, Tara. You have to get it together. We need to leave here. And I need you to not only be on your game but to trust me."

"I did, I mean I do, but—"

"This won't be like your father," he said. "This is us, Tara, we'll make it. I won't lose you again."

"I was safe here," she said as if that resolved everything. Yet she knew that she had no choice. She was the magnet for trouble. To protect him and others, she had to leave here. In the meantime, he had to believe that she was returning to the States with him.

She couldn't endanger anyone again. What had happened today had been her fault. Determination coursed through her. While she couldn't completely agree to what he wanted to do now, she would be there for him later. She'd make the promise now.

"Whatever it takes to get this piece of slime off the streets," she promised. "Whatever it takes to make sure no one else is hurt, I'll do."

"Really?"

She almost smiled at the thought that her words

had been so unexpected as to set him back on his butt. At the least, they took him by surprise.

"I'm a threat to everyone I'm near. People almost died today because of me." She pulled her hands free and touched his arm. "The police can't protect me and you're not in a position to carry a weapon here. This place isn't safe for either of us."

"Exactly," he said and squeezed her hand. "I'll keep you safe in the States. All right?"

"All right," she said in a whisper. With those words she knew that both their destinies had changed but not exactly as he expected. Her palms felt sweaty and she was scared but the decision was made. She was striking out alone—without him.

LUCAS CRUZ SPIT out a string of foul words when he heard the news that Tara Munroe still lived. If nothing else, his brother was at least keeping him posted, but he'd paid his brother for her death. And now Yago was demanding even more. To meet his new demands, Lucas would need to rob more banks. What they'd robbed hadn't been enough. He had two more heists planned in the hopes that would get him the full amount.

Already, the others were griping. He could shut them down. It was Yago he couldn't control. It was imperative that the witness die and soon.

He couldn't believe that she'd escaped again. This was causing him a headache. He wanted desperately to be in San Miguel, but crossing the border would be next to impossible. He had no valid passport and it took time to have a fake one made. Then there was the problem of getting back. Even if he could do all of that, he would still have to actually find her. He was betting that Yago would share none of what he knew with him. That was how things were between them. For now, Lucas was forced to rely on his brother.

He scowled at the thought that all of this was because of a stupid passerby who had somehow outsmarted them all. He wouldn't have it. Bank robbing was evolving into a good deal and there was no way in hell they were going to see it end.

One woman dead before she could yap her pretty face off, and then it would be over. He lived. She died. And he came out rich. You couldn't ask for a better deal than that. It was how life worked. Survival of the fittest.

Chapter Eleven

"There can be no delays," Trent said. He was ready to shut down any resistance she might have. "We leave not tonight or tomorrow morning but now. We'll tell your landlords that you're taking me to Cancún. The deal of the century, short notice, of course, and we're leaving this afternoon. No arguments."

"None. I'm done," she said. "Let's go home." She looked at him without tears. Her words were without emotion.

He'd seen that kind of overwhelmed reaction before. And because of that, he believed her. She lived a quiet life, an artistic life. The last few days must have been a nightmare. Now that she had agreed to go back, he wasn't sure how far he could push her. He didn't know what she thought. Her silence was slightly unnerving. He feared he'd have another argument but this time he knew he'd win. There was no choice.

"So we make an alternative plan. Cancún is the opposite direction and that's where we're going for a little downtime."

"Cancún." She shook her head, not in affirmation or in disagreement but more as if she were trying to wrap her mind around it. "But we don't go."

They were walking back to her apartment as they made the plan.

"Exactly. We leave, but not for Cancún."

"All right," she agreed. There was a quiver in her voice. "You know, I've been here such a short time. Yet I still feel bad about taking off and leaving Carlos and Francesca hanging, wondering what happened to us when we don't come back."

"We'll check out and give them the impression we'll be back but we don't have an exact day, could be a week or two. Our itinerary is so wishy-washy that we have no need of the room being held. Eventually, when this is all over, you can ease their minds and tell them you went home." He shrugged. "They might worry but I think the chances are they'll think you found a better place to vacation or decided to become a beach bum." He smiled at her but there was no answering smile. "They'll be fine. Especially as we're not asking them to hold a room should demand suddenly go up and they want to rent it out to someone else. Taking that into account, you're not doing them any disservice."

He squeezed her hand and she gave a tentative squeeze back. And with that, he believed that the pact was sealed. For better or worse, they were a team.

"So, here are the specifics," he said. "Let's go with my time here is short and you want to show me the beach. We found a deal that flies us out of here later this afternoon. We'll be taking my rental car and leaving it at the airport. In reality we'll be on a flight that should get us home before this time tomorrow."

"It works," she said. "Let me get my head around what I have to tell them."

"And let me worry about the logistics. That's why I'm here. Your only job is to smooth the way with your landlords."

She nodded. As they approached the cobbled steps that led to her apartment, she glanced at him. There was nothing to say. Because of everything that had happened, they were now on the same page. At least on the page that would get her back to the States and into a safe house. He held her hand, as if sealing what they'd just agreed to.

The complex where she rented an apartment was just ahead of them. They went up the stone stairs to the barking of the landlords' dog.

Her landlords were sitting at a table having coffee on the terrace. They both looked up as he and Tara approached. Francesca met their arrival with a smile, while Carlos had a stern expression, as if he wanted to say something but was holding back.

Soon they'd be leaving Mexico far behind. Already, Trent had begun to map out the journey. They'd be heading for the airport in the next hour. Unfortunately, there was no airport within San Miguel's city limits. They would have to drive a short distance to a nearby airport. But that was only a minor problem to work around. The goal was to be on the first flight that took them into the US. At this point it didn't matter what the destination was. The important thing was getting home. Once they landed in the US, they wouldn't be home free but they would be well on their way.

It all sounded so much easier than it was going to be. He knew that. Roadblocks could occur and there was a chance he might not have clear sailing. The men who were hunting her down would expect that she'd flee. The sooner they could leave here, the better their chances.

He stopped, waiting as Tara squatted down to greet a scruffy tricolored dog who scrambled over the cobblestone, barking with obvious joy.

"Hello there, senor," Tara said after a volley of petting. She bent lower to give the dog a hug.

Trent was floored at how quickly she could turn on the charm for a four-legged creature. Especially after everything that she'd been through today. Her fussing over the dog only reminded Trent of who she was when he had known her and of the past they'd once shared. She'd always loved animals and now the little mixed-breed dog danced around until she scooped him up. He couldn't help the memory of the past that seemed to merge with the present. Tara was a talented, bighearted enigma.

He watched as she gave the dog a last scratch on his grizzled head and kissed his chin. Tara acted like all was right with the world. Except, as she set the dog down, her hands shook the slightest amount. He wasn't surprised. She'd been through hell and the day was only half-over.

"Are you all right?" Francesca asked in her heavily accented English as she got up and went to Tara. She hugged her and then held her at arm's length as if searching her for signs of trauma.

Trent liked Francesca and sensed that everything about her was on the up-and-up.

"We heard what happened." Francesca shook her head. "It is all so difficult to fathom, the gangs, the crime, the…" She let Tara's hands go. "Sit, please. We've been watching for you." She ran a hand through her shoulder-length gray-streaked hair. "I was worried sick."

"Where's Siobhan?" Tara asked as she glanced around and saw no sign of her friend.

"Siobhan took a few days off," Francesca replied. "She went to Puerto Vallarta. The opportunity dropped in her lap early this morning. A friend offered her a free flight and she had an hour to decide. She was in a cab to the airport just before all the excitement."

"You'll be shorthanded," Tara said.

Francesca shook her head. "No. It's slow this time of year. Have a seat." She gestured with her hand. "I'll get us some tea."

"No tea, not for me," Trent said. "Thank you."

"Or me," Tara added.

Trent glanced at her and it was like time and life hadn't separated them. A silent communication seemed to run between them. Again, he put his hand over hers. The gesture had seemed to become in a very short time their silent pledge of allegiance. They needed time and they both knew that was what they didn't have.

Chapter Twelve

"I can't believe this all happened literally blocks from our house," Carlos said a few minutes later when they were sitting down at one of a half dozen metal patio tables in the courtyard that was framed by the U-shaped brick building that held the apartments, their landlords' abode and a common kitchen. He threw in a curse for good measure.

"Carlos," Francesca said in a chastising tone.

"I'm sorry, dear, but when my family or guests are in jeopardy I worry, and my language goes south." He leaned forward. His eyes locked with Trent's as if he and Trent were somehow charged with the investigation. "I heard there were shots fired. And you witnessed it? What the hell happened?"

Trent held Tara's hand under the table. He gave it a gentle squeeze before he answered, but still, he could feel the slight tremble. Talking about what happened only brought back the fact that just a few hours ago, she had escaped death.

"There was a gunman. A woman was hit. Fortunately, she should make it." Trent said nothing about Tara being the target. "Unfortunately, he got away."

"There's more that you're not telling me," Carlos said. "I don't blame you but…" He pushed back in his chair. "You can trust me. You should know that I worked for the San Miguel Police. And I can vouch for the fact that this used to be a peaceful place. Of course, that was then. Many places were peaceful back in the day. People were different. Damn, I'm resorting to clichés." He frowned. "And for the most part, it's still pretty peaceful. That's what draws the tourists, the retirees and the artists. Still, the police corruption, the cartels… It has changed. Mostly in other areas but it touches on us once in a while. There's an undercurrent starting to ripple through this town that I don't like. It's not like it used to be when I was working the beat."

Trent nodded. It was information he knew. He'd suspected the truth about the man from the very moment he met him. He'd researched him online in the hours of the night when he couldn't sleep. What he'd found again didn't surprise him.

"I ended my career fifteen years ago as an inspector. Retired early." He shrugged. "The excessive workload and the internal corruption finally did me in. Trust broke at the highest levels. The feds—" He broke off. "I'm sorry, that was a bit of a rant."

"No worries. What about the feds? Anything on them."

"Nothing. Just moldy cop stories." He frowned. "Once a cop, always a cop."

"There is some truth to that," Trent said.

"You knew," Carlos said, reacting to Trent's lack of surprise. "Tara told you?"

"No," Trent said. "But I thought right off that you might have been a police officer." Although that wasn't the whole truth, he'd only guessed. Now he knew, and what he also knew was that despite the time that Carlos had been retired, contacts made in law enforcement could carry forward for years. In every way, law enforcement seemed at all levels and in all countries, at least those he'd seen, to be its own old boys' club.

"We need to talk," Trent said with his gaze focused on the older man. "Privately."

Francesca stood up. "Tara?"

Tara shook her head. "No, Francesca. I sense this is more about me than about anyone else at this table."

Francesca nodded as she turned and walked away, heading toward the apartment she shared with Carlos.

"The police force is worse than it's ever been," Carlos said once the door closed behind his wife. "It wasn't like that in the beginning, when I first joined. But over the twenty years that I was part of it, it slowly devolved. The last few years I was a cop, the department spiraled quickly, and in fact, that was what spurred an early retirement for me. It wasn't so much crime on the street but police willing to take bribes to pad their meager paychecks."

He shook his head. "Good thing I invested well and worked on the side."

He looked into the distance as if contemplating what he wanted to say or how he wanted to say it. "In legitimate ventures," he added. "Legally, there are no financial benefits in a career as a cop in this country. The salaries are low, and the benefits are based on those same salaries or in many areas of the country, completely nonexistent."

He reached for his coffee, held the cup in both hands and then pushed it back. "Look, I've lived in San Miguel for sixty years. That combined with knowledge of how the policing system works here tells me that you have no option. Whatever is going on, whatever you're running from, this morning only proved that you're not going to find safety here."

Trent could feel Tara tense beside him. She hadn't said a word.

"I don't know what you're running from. But I'm guessing whoever is after you has some influence," Carlos said as he looked at Tara. "San Miguel is a great place. It's a quirky place. But it also has an undercurrent of corruption. Whatever you've been caught up in…" He looked at them thoughtfully before going on. "I spoke to one of the officers I know, one of the few I can trust, and he tells me that whoever is after you has ties with a Mexican drug cartel. He was also concerned that they might be offering bribe money for some police support. I can't tell you if that went down or not, or even how many police might be involved. I wish I could tell you more. Do more. But my hands are tied."

Trent muttered and shook his head. This was worse than he'd anticipated.

"I can't have you stay here," Carlos said. "It brings danger and I won't have Francesca put in harm's way for anyone. But I'm guessing you already knew that. Besides, I don't think you should stay anywhere in the area. You need to get out of here, out of the country as quickly as possible."

"I agree. And we were planning to leave," Trent said.

"The sooner the better," Carlos said. "If you go immediately, the cartel won't expect it. If you wait, they will have a contingency plan in place."

"This afternoon," Trent said. "We're gone."

"It's imperative that you stay away from the airports," Carlos said. "The odds that the cartel, the police or someone else is watching are high. They may well have paid someone off to do it. Any way you look at it, they'll have the airports covered." He looked only at Trent, as if Tara was out of the picture when it came to the planning. "Wherever you're going, drive."

Trent shook his head. "No. We'll drive to the airport and—"

"Did you not hear what I just said? The airport is what they'll watch first, all of them. There's no airport near here that will be safe. You have no option but to drive, unless you prefer to be found dead on a Mexican tarmac."

Trent glanced at Tara. She put a hand over her mouth. All thoughts of a ploy to lie about going to

Cancún had become unnecessary. They didn't need to trick her landlords. Carlos didn't know where they were going but he'd minced no words at telling them that they needed to get out.

"How big is this cartel?" That was one of the questions that couldn't be answered on an internet search and that even Jackson had no intel on. There was only the priority system as to how much respect they received. That system was based on how large they were, how feared, how many kills. But they could have any number of nonofficial members jumping to help for what pesos they could get.

"I don't have numbers. From the information I hear off the street, it's small, but the problem is it's growing and quickly. I'm not sure why. Originally, the members were nothing but castoffs from some of the larger cartels but they're coming into their own. That's unfortunate for San Miguel. Seems the police force has allowed some leniency, or shall we say, a little bribery. And I fear now that the cartel is here, they might not leave." Carlos stroked Maxx's head as the dog sat in his lap, eyes half-closed as if there was not a trouble in the world. "Now that you've clashed with them, you're in danger every minute you stay here."

Trent frowned. The news meant driving across the country, which ran a different kind of risk.

He glanced at Tara. Her lips were pressed tightly together. He squeezed her hand.

All thought of a quick flight out vanished. Their travel plans had just become a cross-country drive.

Already, his mind was going through the possibilities. They'd dump electronics. That was a given. He'd seen an atlas in her apartment. It was old-school and exactly what he needed to map out the route that would allow him to bring Tara home. No one could hack an atlas. There was no electronic footprint left on a book.

Trent looked at his watch. "We need to get started."

"You'll make it," Carlos said. "I heard you're one of the best." He stood up with the dog under one arm. "If there's anything else I can do, let me know." He took Tara's hand and kissed it. Then he took Trent's hand and shook it. "It's been nice knowing you both," he said in Spanish. "Godspeed."

He turned and without another word, headed into the main house.

Chapter Thirteen

Trent took Tara's hand. "Let's get moving," he said. "We've got a lot to do and not much time to get it done."

They got to their feet in silence and headed to her apartment. He couldn't imagine the drive ahead. They were about to head out toward an unknown place, a safe house, somewhere in the United States. But first they had to drive across Mexico just to reach the border. Jackson hadn't given him the name of the city where the safe house would be. Trent would get that information once they crossed the border. For now, he could only assume that the safe house was set up and that it was there, waiting for them. He could be wrong. And if he was, it didn't matter. He'd deal with it when or if the problem presented itself.

He was out of communication for now and had to focus on one thing: getting Tara out of Mexico. Tara had already ditched her phone when she'd ran from her home and everything that was familiar. And considering all that had happened, he was now ditching his. They were in an electronic blackout from here on.

He would rely on Enrique, but he didn't trust the local police. There had been something off when they had questioned him earlier. He didn't plan to give them any further information. For now, he'd check in with Enrique and Jackson only as needed. It was the safest way to go.

Although they'd no longer have their phones, Tara's past visits to San Miguel de Allende, recorded on social media, were still retrievable to the best hackers. He assumed the cartel knew someone who fell in that category. They'd clearly found her and now she had to disappear again.

"How long?" she asked.

He knew without her saying more that she was asking how long before they needed to leave the apartment. "As soon as possible. Thirty minutes," he said. "Can you do it?"

"I'm going to have to."

They would head north, taking as direct a route as possible and hitting the border without delay.

He opened the door to the apartment and Tara paused in the doorway.

"You saved my life," she whispered. And then her arms were around his neck like they had been so many years ago, and she was kissing him.

It was unlike any kiss that had come before. The body that was pressed against him was that of a woman, not a girl. And he was no longer a boy and hadn't been for many years. He was one broken engagement, a cluster of ended relationships and a dozen years past his boyhood. But all the trouble and the years that had fallen between them were erased as the kiss went from soft to hot and hard.

It was a kiss that drew a man in and made him never want to let go. It was a kiss that made him hard and crazy. One that made him forget everything that was important for a precious minute, including getting her the hell out of Mexico.

The kiss ended as quickly as it had begun, it seemed almost by mutual agreement. The decision only leaving a memory of the passion they'd shared and a yearning for more. He felt it in his heart and saw the shared emotion in her eyes and in the touch of her hand on his shoulder.

As much as he'd like to see this through, they both knew they had to get moving. But to do that he needed a plan—a solid thought-out plan that took him from here and finally back home. There was no room for screwing up. Simply getting over the border wasn't enough. He needed resources in place and somewhere to hide once they got there. But first he had to get there. The truth was that if he didn't come up with a plan, get them packed and get them out of here in the next half hour, she might die. They had no idea how little time they had before someone else would be after her. That was all the motivation he needed.

"Can I help?" she asked.

"No." He shook his head and laid a hand on her arm. "It will work out, Tara. I'll get you home safely."

"I'll get packed," she said but there was something in her voice that made him look up. Her chin quivered. He was afraid that she was about to burst into tears.

"Tara."

"I'm sorry. It's just all hitting me. I know that sounds strange but it's finally becoming real." The words trembled on her lips and she looked frightened.

He was on his feet and had his arms around her before she could say another word. Her body shook—hit by shock, he assumed. What she'd experienced—the trauma of being shot at, of having the danger that threatened her—must have been terrifying. Especially for anyone not trained to deal with such things.

"We'll get you home, don't worry."

She gave him a half smile that was less confident than her words. "I never doubted you, Trent." And then she went into the bedroom and he could hear the thump of her bag as she began to pack her things.

He sat down with the atlas on his lap.

Ten minutes passed. He looked up to see Tara in the doorway, a knapsack in hand. She was packed but he wasn't yet ready to go. He needed to brief her. He wanted her fully on board, fully aware of the details. They had a cartel after them. He had to have her prepared for the worst-case scenario, the possibility that they would get separated. It wouldn't happen, but he had to prepare her for the possibility that she might be left alone. That way, she could continue the way he had mapped and eventually get home.

"Let me show you the route we're taking."

She sat down beside him as if this was nothing out of the ordinary. A few minutes later, he'd shown her exactly what he'd planned. "At least, that's what I have so far."

"Thank you for doing that," she said. "It helps to be involved."

"I thought it might," he said, although that hadn't been the reason for telling her. There was no need for more specifics. There'd been enough fear in her life today. "You're ready?"

"Yes," she replied. "I hate leaving like this."

"Carlos has as much as told us to leave. And without formally dropping off your key, he and Francesca can truthfully say we skipped on them and they have no idea when we left or where we went. Remember we can update them later, like we discussed. When this is over."

There was a doubtful look in her eye. So he went in for the argument that he knew would clinch his win. "For now, they already know more than I'd like. Leaving unannounced will be the best way to protect them. I know you don't like the idea of just leaving, of not thanking them."

The look she gave him was one he couldn't interpret. Not then. It was only later that he realized that much of what she'd said, her agreement, all of it—had been a ruse.

Chapter Fourteen

Tara stood in the bathroom doorway, her hand on the doorknob. She tried her best to appear cooperative. She'd listened as he'd mapped a route that he thought would eventually take them home. She also knew how methodical he was. He would have the lines of the map memorized.

She hated herself for what she was about to do but she had no choice. She'd used some of Siobhan's foundation to make her face appear pale and she was doing her best to look pained. She took a deep breath. This ploy had to work.

She was terrified that it wouldn't.

It had to.

She couldn't allow Trent to risk his life. What had happened this morning couldn't happen again. He could have died in the process of protecting her. She couldn't have that on her conscience. The thought of that, of something happening to him, something happening to another man in her life was unbearable. She wouldn't let it happen this time, not when she could do something about it.

But Trent was not the man in her life. The boy that he'd been was long gone. She'd loved and lost since then. Now they were together in a different way. He was her protector—no more. And yet, despite everything, her heart said otherwise.

She needed to focus. The priority was making sure that he wasn't hurt or killed because of her. To do that, she had to leave. She had to get away from him, away from San Miguel. She needed to get far away and yet nowhere near home and the States. Somewhere she wasn't known. Where she couldn't be found. More important, where she wouldn't endanger anyone and where she could disappear, whether that meant moving and staying or remaining on the move until this was over. She hadn't figured that out yet. All she knew was that she'd be leaving San Miguel—alone.

"Tara," Trent said as he turned, his blue eyes dark with worry. "What's wrong?" A hand was on her forearm, a frown between his brows.

"I have a killer headache." She kept her voice low with little inflection. Would he believe her when only minutes ago she was kissing him with all the passion she felt for him in her heart?

"I'll get you some aspirin," he said with a look of concern. "I've got some in my bag."

"No." She shook her head. "That doesn't work. I get migraines often and that might be where this is going." She was dredging up symptoms from memory and what she'd been told by a girlfriend who suffered from debilitating migraines. "It should clear up once I've lain down for a bit. I'm just afraid that it could turn into a full-blown migraine and I could be puking sick."

She realized that using the term *puking sick* might have been pushing things. But she needed him out of here long enough for her to implement her exit strategy. She needed a good head start to get on a bus and get out of town. This time she was sure that he wouldn't be able to find her. She'd post nothing on social media. The mistakes of her recent past were well learned and remembered. She'd run in a blind panic, and she'd paid for her mistake. She had to disappear so deep that Trent would never find her until it was safe and then she'd return on her own.

Regret ran deep through her—she knew that he'd feel used. He'd think that she'd kissed him without feeling anything for him, that she'd played on his emotions. But that wasn't how it was. She'd felt the depths of that kiss to her soul. And felt the pain of losing him again more poignantly than she had the first time.

"I hate this. I endanger you all," she murmured.

"No…"

She held up her hand. "Don't, Trent. There's nothing you can say. We both know the truth. People almost died because of me and one woman was injured. Who knows what pain she's suffered because of me."

She pressed her fingers to her temple, massaging them as if to ease the pain.

"Is there anything that might help?"

"There is something that works—not all the time. But nothing else touches it." She mentioned a pain-killer that she was pretty sure he didn't carry.

"I'll get it," he said, standing up. He looked at his watch. "We need to be on the road I'd say by three at the outside. Do you think you can make it?"

"If you have to, carry me," she said. "Seriously, if I get the medication before it turns into a full-blown migraine, I should be okay in an hour."

"There's a pharmacy a few blocks away. I'll be right back."

"I'll lie down while you're gone. Thanks."

She stared at the door for a good minute after he closed it. She doubted after what she was about to do that he'd ever want to see her again. And as a result, she wished that she could say so much more. Instead, *thanks* had to be all. He'd never know but it was thanks for so many things.

For being there for her and saving her life this morning. For the beautiful kiss and the promise of a romance that, again, could never be. Risking his life to protect her was unthinkable but he'd done it. She wouldn't have him do it again. He'd already done so much. The most she could do was protect him by getting out of his life and leading the danger away from him.

She left him a note explaining why he needed to return home. Explaining that she was safe and that there was no need to worry. She promised to con-tact him when she got to her destination. It was the best she could do, but whether he searched for her or not, he wouldn't be with her. And that alone was a much safer option.

The second hand on the wall clock ticked away another minute and then another two. At the five-minute mark, she grabbed the atlas and shoved it into her knapsack, slinging the bag over her shoulder. She opened the door he'd closed so recently and breathed in a sigh of relief.

The courtyard was empty. Siobhan was gone and there were no other tenants. There were only her landlords and she hoped they remained inside. Her hand shook as she closed the door, thinking of what could have happened if it hadn't been for Trent.

Trent. She owed him so much. Protecting him was the least that she could do.

"Goodbye," she whispered. She stood there for a few seconds that seemed so much longer. She didn't move, just breathed, garnering the courage to go ahead with what needed to be done. If all went well, the next time she saw him would be in court. When or how that would play out, she didn't know.

Carlos had already outlined what he thought the cartel would do. Following the local bus wasn't one of the things he'd mentioned.

She looked at her watch. It was one thirty. The bus left in thirty minutes. She'd checked on that yesterday before Trent had arrived.

To her, Guadalajara had always seemed, because of its size, a good place to disappear and figure things out. She'd planned to be there for a few days and then she'd be off again, possibly heading south. Last night, after drinks with Siobhan and Trent she'd retired to her closet-size bedroom, where she'd considered her options and mapped out a number of routes before settling on this one. She'd never planned to stay in San Miguel de Allende anyway. She'd known that she'd eventually have to leave. The only change since Trent had arrived, and the incident this morning, was that she was leaving sooner.

It was time to move on, alone. She squared her shoulders and headed to the steps at the back of the property. They led to a narrow residential street. From there, it wasn't a long walk to the bus depot.

When Trent returned and found that she was gone, he might be angry, but he would no longer be in danger. He would look for her. But he wouldn't find her. Because of that he wouldn't die.

Unlike her father, he would live.

Chapter Fifteen

Trent had the package of medication in his hand and was ten feet from Tara's apartment when Carlos called to him.

"Trent, can I speak to you?"

He didn't hesitate—Carlos knew the urgency of their situation. He wouldn't delay him for anything that wasn't extremely important. He sat down across from Carlos at an outside table.

"I just wanted to give you a heads-up. I thought you might need some help, so I got in touch with someone I know with the feds. He had some information in regard to which routes might be the safest and fastest to get to the US border and avoid areas where the cartels have become problematic. I don't know what your plan is but if you're going home, watch these areas." He pointed to highways on the map he'd brought with him, those north of San Miguel de Allende and some of the roads heading west. "There's been a lot of violence, tourist kidnappings, a laundry list of crap happening that way. The cartels have been busy. I'd advise dodging the area.

Your best bet would be to take the main highway to here." He tapped the map. "Come around the west side of Guadalajara. Then from there, take this road. It's mostly used by farm workers, and there isn't a lot of traffic, but it heads north and eventually connects with a main highway." He ran his finger along a route that would take them straight to the border. "If you run into problems, let me know. Maybe I can help."

"I'll pick up a disposable phone along the way, in case I need to reach out to anyone," Trent replied.

Five minutes later, Trent entered Tara's apartment and went immediately to the closed bedroom door. He knocked once, twice, and waited.

No answer.

He guessed that Tara was sleeping. He glanced at his watch. They were tight on time. He had no choice but to wake her; they had to get going soon. He hoped that the painkiller would help and that she could sleep while they were driving. He knocked once more and opened the door.

The room was empty.

He swore a litany of words, some of which he hadn't used in years.

He'd been gone twenty minutes. He'd shaved five minutes off his time by jogging the entire way back from the pharmacy. He'd even ignored the offer of a bag. He wasn't wasting a second in getting back to her. Except for the few critical moments with Carlos. And now she wasn't here. The apartment was empty. He backed out of the tiny room and looked around.

His knapsack sat where he'd left it. Her bag and the atlas were gone.

He didn't need to search the property any further. He knew she wasn't there. He also knew that her claim of a headache had been the perfect decoy, coming out of the blue like it had. But there'd been other hints and he'd missed them all. The way she hadn't questioned anything about his plans to get them out of San Miguel. He'd showed her the route. Now her total lack of curiosity was only a foreshadowing of what was to come.

He'd missed all the clues, including what she had said before he'd headed for the pharmacy. When she'd been faking her headache. It was a neon light in hindsight.

I hate this. I endanger you all.

He spewed another flood of curses that changed nothing. He looked at the counter and saw a small piece of paper. He picked it up and saw his name at the top. He quickly scanned the note and then read it again.

He was shaking his head when he was done. She'd gotten it all wrong. She didn't need to run to protect him and he sure as hell wasn't returning home as she'd suggested. As far as where she planned to head—he took no account to that. He knew right off she was trying to misdirect him. The most the note had done was convince him what direction not to go to find her. He could only hope she hadn't had much of a head start.

He ran outside. He looked to the main street;

nothing. He turned instead to a side staircase that led to a narrow back street. He stood at the top, his gaze sweeping the area. There was nothing except a man in the distance with a wheelbarrow and a small pack of stray dogs.

He was too late. But if he thought about it, she would have run as soon as he'd left. That gave her close to a thirty-minute jump on him. If that was the case, she could be anywhere. All he had was the knowledge that she hadn't stayed here in San Miguel. Apparently, he thought grimly, that was the only thing that they had agreed on.

He knew she was trying to protect him and the others around her. The thought of that when protection was his job was beyond insulting. Of course, he knew that she hadn't meant it like that. He knew she was always concerned about others and this was only an extension of her personality. Still, he was frustrated and angry, not at her but at himself. He should have picked up on this. He should have known. And he never should have left her and given her this kind of opportunity.

He glanced at his watch. He'd wasted a minute in a situation where he had no time to waste. He needed to spend the time getting inside her head and figuring out where she was headed. Blaming anyone, including himself, wasn't going to get either of them anywhere. There was no changing the past.

She'd agreed to everything too easily. He knew that now. He'd completely believed the headache. He'd seen how pale she'd looked. He'd never thought twice that she wasn't sick. He'd never even considered that she might be faking it. She'd hoodwinked him. He'd fallen for one of the oldest tricks in the book.

"Damn it."

But something had bothered him from the beginning. Mainly it had been a fear for her safety. Although they'd felt like a team, he'd feared losing her. He couldn't explain the fear for he'd never felt anything like that before. But, because of it, he'd planted the bug in her knapsack more as a precaution to keep her safe, than as a sign of mistrust. Now he was glad that he had done that.

Trent grabbed his go bag. He pulled out the receiver. It had a signal, and from the looks of things, she had a twenty-five-mile jump on him. The next time he looked, it was thirty. It could be a tech glitch or it could mean that wherever she was, she'd hit the highway. She was moving too fast to be in the city or on foot. And he still had to get through the tight city streets.

She'd boarded a bus. That was an easy conclusion. Yesterday, Trent had run a check on her finances. He doubted if she'd take what little money she had and fly. Flying also involved identification, and with Carlos's earlier warnings to dodge airports, that clinched the fact that she'd stuck to land. He could only hope that would also make her an easy find.

Five minutes later, he was in his rental car and heading through San Miguel's tight streets. It was an arduous process; traffic was backed up because of an accident. He banged the steering wheel in frustration as cars crawled along. Finally, he came to an intersection where he was able to veer off. But that posed a convoluted drive as well before he was finally out of the city and on the highway.

"Why didn't you listen to me?" he seethed as he smacked the steering wheel yet again.

But he knew why. She looked after everyone, including those charged with looking after her. It was why she'd given him the headache story and then run. By leaving him behind, she probably felt that she was protecting him. Unfortunately, by the law of averages, her luck was running thin.

He needed to find her before it was too late.

Chapter Sixteen

Tara clutched her knapsack. It was all she had in the world. She was alone in this and she had to get used to that fact. She couldn't put any more lives in jeopardy. Most important, she needed to put distance between herself and the men who were after her. From here on, she couldn't make friends or get close to anyone and she had to keep on the move—at least for now.

She'd boarded the bus only blocks from where she'd stayed in San Miguel. Unfortunately, the bus was full of locals and as a foreigner, she stood out, making her memorable. As soon as she had a chance, she would have to change her look. Eventually she planned to disappear, either in this country or another. She'd hide until the time came for her to testify. She'd yet to figure out how she'd know when that would be. For now, it was one problem at a time.

Her thoughts were broken by the antics of a small boy ahead of her. He peeked over the seat and pointed his finger at her like he had a toy gun. She gave him a smile as the woman beside him whispered to him and he turned and sat back down. She was still smiling as she scanned the bus. She couldn't afford to be complacent; it was just her and she needed to make sure she was safe.

Across the aisle, two women were sitting together and chatting in Spanish. Her high school grasp of the language allowed her to catch only simple phrases and the occasional word. She looked away as the boy peeked over the seat again and smiled at her. A few rows up, someone was humming under their breath. She looked out the window. She wasn't sure where she was going or where she would be safe. Was anywhere safe? Would they find her no matter what she did or where she went?

Buck up, she told herself. *You're tougher than this. You can keep yourself safe for as long as necessary. Whether you have to go farther south or no matter what you have to do, you can do it.*

But could she?

She'd run from a gunman. She'd been terrified. Unlike Trent, who had chased an armed man unarmed. He was a hero and she was running from him. But she couldn't endanger him or others. She needed to get away. But she couldn't fool herself, she was no hero. Not like Trent.

She thought of him in ways she hadn't in a long time. Except it was no longer the love of a girl but...

She frowned. She couldn't think of him like that. She couldn't consider what might have been. And yet it was impossible not to. He'd matured into a man who could make any woman look twice. Beautiful blue eyes and full lips with a square jaw that seemed to speak of determination. He had classic good looks; even as a youth, he'd had a killer physique, but now he seemed even more physically imposing. Combine that with a gentleness that could morph quickly into tough guy, and he was magnetic.

"Stop it," she whispered to herself. *Stop thinking about him as if he were part of your life. It's over. It was over a long time ago.*

She looked out the window as the bus pulled into a service station on the edges of a village. It was a push to call the place a village; it was really no more than a cluster of shanty houses. A couple got off and two men got on. They wore faded jeans and bland beige-and-white T-shirts without even a logo to brighten them. The T-shirts hung too big on both of them. Despite the temperature, one had a faded tan jacket slung over his shoulder. It was as if he was hiding something, and yet that thought didn't ring any warnings. It wasn't like anyone on this bus was dressed to the nines or hitting any fashion trends.

She half smiled at the thought as she watched the two men sit down in the seat behind the driver. Another five minutes passed. Tara pulled out the atlas. The bus was heading to Guadalajara. Trent would never think that she had gone there. It was the opposite direction of where she should go if she didn't want to go back to the States for that was where the crime had happened and that was where the criminals still were. They wanted her dead and despite the fact that it seemed no safer here, at least it was farther from the place where she'd witnessed the robbery and from where her home had been violated as they'd looked for her. Besides being in another country, Guadalajara was at least big enough and touristy enough that it might be a perfect place to disappear into. It was only temporary. A place where she could come up with a more solid plan than the current one.

Her thoughts were broken by men's angry voices. The words were incomprehensible, but so harsh that they sent a shiver through her.

She looked up. At the front, one of the two men who had recently got on the bus was standing. He had a gun aimed at the driver. The second man had a gun waving left and then right, taking in all of them.

Tara froze—stunned. A woman screamed. For a minute, she couldn't believe what she was seeing, couldn't digest it. She almost forgot to breathe before her mind kicked back into gear. Was it her who they were after?

The possibility hit in a tsunami of fright. The atlas slid to the floor. She froze, her right hand clutching a piece of leather that dangled from the worn seat as if it were a lifeline.

As the seconds passed and no one looked at her and as one gunman continued to focus on the driver, his older partner smirked at them all. It was becoming clear that this might not be about her. That was somewhat of a relief as the bus slowed and stopped at the side of the road. There was a cacophony of voices as passengers panicked. Her assumption was proving itself; there was no search of the bus. It was like they didn't care who the passengers were.

Then what was this about? Her mind ran through the options. A simple robbery? Her heart leaped in panic. No matter what their motive, there was nothing simple about this. They were all in danger. They could all die.

"What do you want?" a man's voice asked.

Tara didn't know if it was the driver who spoke or one of the few men who were on the bus. She was too far back and couldn't get a clear view. What she could see between the heads of the other passengers was a man who might be in his forties, was shorter than the other and seemed to be leading the assault.

"Shut up!" he shouted in Spanish as he pointed his gun. He waved it across the rows, threatening them all in general.

Tara froze. The weapon mesmerized her. The man was holding a semiautomatic Beretta. A similar gun, of all the guns in his vast collection, had been a favorite of her grandfather's.

The thought was fleeting in the midst of this drama. She dragged her eyes away from the gun and for a second it seemed that hard eyes looked right at her. Then a woman stood and blocked Tara's view. Half the bus was standing now and there was quiet chaos. It was impossible to see much.

She caught a glimpse of the other man, aiming at the driver. He was in his twenties, holding what her grandfather called a straight-shooting poor man's gun. It was a battered, sawed-off shotgun. The weapon fitted his sullen swarthy face, his dark attitude. He turned, the jacket was gone, and in the gap of panicked passengers, their eyes met. His were full of distrust and hate and sent a chill through Tara. And then, just like that, her view was gone. He was hidden by the other passengers.

Tara hoped this would all end peacefully. Ahead there was the literal threat of death. Her hands were clenched so hard that her knuckles were white.

"Don't move," one of the men shouted in Spanish. "No one move," he repeated as he brandished his weapon.

Tara sucked back a panicked breath, and her fingernails dug into her palms. For a minute she forgot to breathe. The nightmare had just gone from bad to worse.

TRENT GLANCED AT the receiver. She was steadily moving away from San Miguel. And then everything stopped.

Perhaps her bus had stopped to pick up passengers.

Minutes passed. He was twenty miles away now and still she hadn't moved.

At ten miles, she was still in the same position. If he'd been right about the bus, it would have left a big center and would be stopping to pick up passengers. Each stop would be roadside and a matter of minutes, at least so he assumed, if the bus wanted to keep on schedule. But the pace in the rural areas could be slow.

Still, he was concerned. Maybe she wasn't on a bus at all. If that was the case, he was at a loss as to what was going on.

Five miles, no movement. Had she dropped her knapsack for some reason? The thought of that sent chills through him, for that meant deeper trouble.

His foot rode heavier on the gas pedal, picking up speed, feeling the urgency. Finally, he was there, and he had a visual.

A local bus was pulled over at the side of the road with not a town or village in sight. Add to that, it was angled with its nose partway in the ditch, as if the driver had been under the influence of something or someone, and that all spelled definite trouble. He drove by as if there was nothing suspicious. But that thought was quickly killed when he saw the shadow of a man at the front of the bus and then clearly, the gun in his hand.

His fingers tightened on the wheel as he kept driving. He only pulled over when the road made a slight curve and hid him from sight of those on the bus.

What the hell, he thought as he got quietly out of the car. His mind spun through the possibilities and prepared to be faced with the worst-case scenario, whatever that might be. He wished to hell that he had his Beretta 92 at his side or, for that matter, any of the dozens of guns in his collection. Instead, the only weapon he had was himself. It would have to be enough.

Chapter Seventeen

Tara's fright was spinning into anger. At this point, she wasn't sure which emotion to go with. She hated what was happening. And she hated the fact that she could do nothing about it. She glared from her seat. But no one could see her and it would be foolish to draw attention to herself. There were too many lives at stake. The bus had been half-empty when it left San Miguel. Now almost every seat was full. There was a woman with a baby and a toddler in the seat in front of her, and an elderly couple a few seats up—and now this.

The two gunmen were still closer to the front as they roared their commands. Dressed in clothes meant to blend in, the only thing that stood out now were the guns each of them held.

She glanced to her left and up a row. The baby had been wailing since the first gunshot had taken out the front window.

Now one man was going row by row, taking what valuables each passenger had. The other stood with a gun still aimed at the driver. The message was clear: one act of resistance, and the driver would die. There was nothing they could do without jeopardizing his life.

A woman gave a little cry as the man tried to rip a ring off her finger.

"¡Cállate a todos!" the older man roared, his thin face seeming even harder, the wrinkles even more pronounced.

Tara's high school Spanish told her what he demanded. *Shut up! All of you.*

She wasn't planning to say anything. Instead, her teeth were clenched so tight that her jaw hurt. She watched as the smaller man ripped a woman's bag from her side and rifled through it. He yanked out a wallet and then threw the bag down.

She slid lower in her seat as she watched for an opportunity, something she could do to stop them. But as the pair made their way down the aisle, she began to quiver. She was still the only Caucasian on the bus. The rest were all locals. She stood out and in a situation like this, that wasn't a good thing. They could pull her out, make her an example.

"Dinero, joyas, dánoslo," the larger of the two shouted as he waved his gun from side to side. He shouted this at regular intervals, as if they needed any kind of reminder.

Money, jewelry, give it to us, she translated the words in her head. Yeah, she'd like to give it to him all right, Tara thought, her fists clenched. She'd like to use her fist and hit him right in his smirking face.

A middle-aged woman a few seats ahead shifted,

perching on her seat. It was like she was ready for action, to somehow jump in and do something about it all. Across the aisle, an older man seemed to be sitting taller, straighter than the others, as if he, too, was ready to jump in when the opportunity presented itself.

Tara hunched down but every muscle was taut, readying herself to do whatever needed to be done to get them out of this. She wasn't sure what she could do, but if there was an opportunity, she wasn't going to miss it. And yet something curdled deep in her stomach, knowing since this all began that they could all be looking death in the face. She'd heard stories of such robberies, how criminals got off on their victims' fear. In those cases, even after getting everything they wanted, they killed.

The thought had barely registered its chilling reality when everything changed.

Chaos was erupting around her. A toddler burst into screeching cries and the baby howled louder. People stood up, blocking her view. Screams seemed to echo through the interior as everything devolved further.

Tara's heart was in her throat as she feared the worst. She couldn't see through the crush of people as passengers were out of their seats. The roar of gunfire again almost deafened her. The side window near the front was blown out and glass flew everywhere.

The gunmen screamed orders to sit or die. And most of the passengers sat. She wished they hadn't.

She was still standing when she once again met the dark gaze of one of the gunmen. She froze and then sat as he turned and fired a shot that took out another side window.

It was then that she caught a glimpse of a man she would know anywhere. Her heart tripped and she knew that the robbers had yet to see him, for if they had, they would have done more than take out another window. Apparently taking out the window had been pure theatrics since, from what she could see, it gained them nothing.

Trent.

She'd recognize that hair, that face in any crowd, in any place. He was there and then he was gone. He was outside, coming around the front of the bus. He'd come out of nowhere, maybe out of the ditch, she didn't know where, but he was like an answer to a prayer.

And he needed help so he wouldn't be noticed. He needed a diversion.

Tara screamed and ducked down, grabbing the atlas from the floor and rising up to bang it against the glass again and again. She hoped that no one got killed because of this and that the distraction took their attention to the back of the bus long enough for him to do what needed to be done.

"Get down!" she shouted. She screamed it over and over again in English and Spanish until a bullet winged over her head and one of the men shouted for silence.

She was quiet then. She sat on the edge of her seat

as her heart pounded. She could see to the front of the bus for her screaming had done one thing: everyone sat or hunkered way down in their seat. For a second, she was frozen in fear, in disbelief and in hope. Her diversion had worked.

Trent was on the bus.

Then he was a blur of motion. One moment, there were two men with guns, and the next moment, one of them was screaming with his arm twisted behind his back. His gun skidded down the aisle and out of sight. It all happened so fast that the second man didn't have a chance to move before Trent gave him a lightning-fast kick to the knees and he fell hard with a small shriek of pain.

Tara gasped and put a hand to her mouth.

A woman to her left and a few seats up slid out of her seat and ducked down. A second later she was up, the first man's gun in both hands.

She saw a flash of movement as the second gunman got up on one good leg. His free hand slammed the woman's, knocking the gun free. The weapon flew again, landing in the aisle, sliding away.

Trent still had the other man's arm wrenched behind his back while two male passengers grabbed the second and threw him back to the ground.

Trent pushed the first one forward, throwing him off balance. The woman who had picked up one of the guns and had it knocked from her hands, now had retrieved it and had it aimed at the robber's head.

Trent moved further into the bus, planting his foot on the second one's throat. "Move and die," he snarled. He looked over to where a middle-aged man now held the sawed-off shotgun.

"You've got this?" Trent asked him in Spanish and then looked behind him at the woman who had retrieved the other gun.

"Sí," they both replied.

Another woman stood up. She waved her phone. "The police are on their way," she said in Spanish.

Two passengers, two guns. And each of them had a gun trained on one of the would-be thieves, who had threatened not only to rob but kill.

Trent strode toward her. "You're all right?" he asked as the palm of his hand ran the curve of her cheek.

She nodded and stood up. She was too stunned to do anything but put her hand in his. She quietly followed as he led her to the front of the bus.

"I'll be right back," he said in Spanish to the driver. "I've got something that will hold these two."

Outside, he led her to his car, parked some distance away. He let go of her hand as he opened the trunk and took out some rope.

"Wait here," he said. "I'll be right back."

Two minutes later, he'd returned. "They're tied up and the police are on their way. There's nothing more I can do."

"You saved my life again," she said in a whisper. It was all she could think to say.

She'd stood waiting for him, leaning against the trunk and wondering what she would do without him. For the first time, doubt set in. She couldn't do this alone. The hazards of this country, combined with the threat that was for her alone, were more than she could overcome. She was an amateur. He'd been right all along. There was no disputing the fact that he was good at what he did. He'd defeated odds in a situation that was unimaginable. This kind of danger, the kind she'd faced today alone, was beyond anything she could have comprehended a week ago.

"You're okay?"

"Yes." She nodded. "Thanks to you. Thank you."

"It's what I do," he said, confirming her earlier thoughts. He took her arm. "Let's you and me get out of here. They'll be fine." He nodded toward the other passengers. "And the authorities have more than enough witnesses to the crime. The police will be here soon, and we can't afford any more delays."

He held the car door open for her. It was the rental car that she knew had already taken him through a good chunk of Mexico to find her.

"Should I give you hell for running on me now or…?" he asked.

The quivers stopped at his words and were replaced by outrage. "Don't you dare, Trent Nielsen. Don't you dare. You shouldn't have followed me." She was being outrageous, and she knew it. He'd saved her life—again. To add to that, he'd saved the lives of twenty other people. He was a hero and she was treating him like dirt.

She was all over the map and she could only say it was because she was terrified. Terrified for him, for what he did to her. And she was doing her best to push him away. She'd endangered too many people already, including him.

"That's not what I meant," he began, his voice soft.

"Go home, Trent," she said. "Go back to the States. This is my problem. Let me handle it. Please." She knew even as she said it that she was being ridiculous. She'd proved in less than two hours that she was capable all right, capable of putting herself in a mess with no way out.

"I can't. I won't go home without you."

"No." She shook her head.

"Yes." He took both her hands in his. "Eventually, I'll get you to Colorado, where you belong but for now, until that happens, you are my home."

Her heart raced at his words for they almost brought her to her knees.

Chapter Eighteen

"Get in."

There was nothing harsh in his voice. He could tell by the look she gave him that she'd taken no offense. They both knew that the time for niceties was over. They needed to get the hell out of here, fast. Already his mind was running through the options. He hit on one place. *Hide in plain sight.* The more he thought of the option, the more it became the most viable. At least for tonight.

She got into his car, her knapsack slung over her shoulder.

"Wait. Give me your bag," he said. He didn't wait for her reply but instead he slipped it off her arm before she had a chance to react.

"Hey!" she objected. "It has all my stuff…"

She stopped. Her eyes were dark with disbelief. He glanced only once. He could feel the heat of her glare. He opened her pack and pulled out the device that had brought him here. He threw it into the ditch. When he turned back with the bag in his hand, he met her wrath.

"What the hell? You had me tracked. I can't believe it." The look she gave him was one of surprise and betrayal.

"And you'd be dead if I hadn't," he said.

He wished he hadn't been so blunt, but his words had the intended effect. She didn't say a thing.

"We need to get moving," he said in the face of her silence. He'd explain later. But in the meantime, he hated letting her believe that he'd tracked her for all the wrong reasons.

The authorities were on their way and the last thing he needed was to be here when they arrived. There would be questions that would take them nowhere and help no one. They would have all their answers on that bus. He needed to get her away from here without further delay.

Seconds later he pulled onto the highway heading in the direction of San Miguel de Allende.

"We're going back? No, Trent. We can't—"

He could see that her anger was gone and was now replaced by panic.

"No." He cut her off with a shake of his head. "You're right. You can never go back."

He sensed her confusion. He didn't blame her for what he'd said and what he was doing was contradictory. His eyes never left the road as he said, "We're laying a false trail by stopping at a few places before we turn around. Then we'll get off this route and head to the Lake Chapala area. We can blend in there, at least for tonight. Unfortunately, I'm winging that. It wasn't part of the plan—any plan."

"It's familiar," she said.

He nodded. Chapala was Mexico's biggest inland lake. Villages and towns stretched out along its shores. The population consisted of Mexicans as well as Americans and Canadians. In fact, it was a popular retirement and travel destination, especially for Canadian snowbirds. For tonight, they would go unnoticed in such an environment.

"The tracking device was in case we were separated. I meant to tell you. But there was never time. I wouldn't have found you otherwise."

Their eyes met and there was a spark in hers, a tremble of her lips the only sign of the trauma she'd escaped. "Brilliant, Trent," she said but there was still a quiver in her voice. "For you found me in the end. Now, I have a confession. The atlas didn't make it." She explained what she'd used it for and how it was left on the bus.

It was dusk when they hit the fringes of Lake Chapala. They stopped at a small worn inn where they checked in and left their few belongings in the main floor room that was also close to an exit. The inn met Trent's requirements. He'd listed them to her on the drive. More to keep her entertained, she thought, than to keep her informed. It was a place where the owner asked for none of the usual identification or credit or debit card payments. Trent wanted none of the hoopla of a larger hotel. The place couldn't have been any more perfect.

She'd set her knapsack down on the luggage rack and was now perched on the edge of one twin bed.

"I'm sorry, Trent. I screwed up. There was never a reason to run."

He glanced at her with surprise. He hadn't expected that. "In your shoes, I don't know if I would have believed that my plan was the best either."

"Now I know that I can't do this alone. I don't know what I'm doing. It was crazy to run. Stupid even. I'm not my father."

"It's done, and no one is the worse because of it," he replied, skating over the reference to her father, who had died in witness protection. He took her hand and squeezed it.

"I didn't want to endanger you."

He almost laughed at the statement. From anyone else, it would have been insulting. From her, it wasn't. He knew she was stressed, exhausted and more than likely didn't have a clue what she'd just said. "It's what I do. In some circles, I'm even considered good at it." He glanced at her. "All your running on me has done is set us hours behind."

"I didn't want you to be hurt. It's me they're after. I thought—"

"I should have been one step ahead. It's my job and you outmaneuvered me." But she'd always been too smart for her own good. It was what he'd loved about her, that and so many other things. He pushed those thoughts from his mind. They were irrelevant.

"No," she whispered in a shaky voice bringing his mind back to the conversation at hand. "I was stupid, arrogant even, to think I could go it alone."

This wasn't where he wanted this to go. There

was no room for chastisement. He needed her on her game, with him and not blinded by a pity party. Bad things happened, and they needed to move on. He glanced at his watch. It was eight o'clock in the evening.

"Are you hungry?" he asked. It was a stupid question as his stomach rumbled. They hadn't eaten all day. There hadn't been time for it.

"Starving," she said with relief in her voice.

He glanced at her. Her face was pale. Her jaw was set. She looked at him with determination in her eyes.

"Then let's grab something to eat," he said. His stomach rumbled again. It was as if what to eat was the most important thing he needed to decide, as if they were on vacation rather than on the run.

Once on the narrow sidewalk that bordered an equally narrow street, he took her hand, telling himself that would make them look more like any other couple out for a stroll. In reality, the heat that streaked through him at the feel of her flesh against his only made him want her more. Only made him want her in every way.

But such thoughts were outrageous and dangerous. He had to be alert. Especially here, on the street. Lake Chapala might appear safe, but appearances could be deceiving.

"Here," she said as they passed a restaurant with tables set out on the sidewalk.

It was a relief to have those thoughts broken. He smiled at her. She reciprocated and grabbed his arm, pulling him over to take a closer look. The food smelled good and the menu board told him it would be affordable. Her nod told him everything he needed to know.

A minute later they were sitting across from each other. But any hope of conversation ended as a pair of guitarists began playing on the nearby boardwalk. Still, the music compensated for its volume by actually being good, and Tara claimed that the outdoor pizza bar was perfection when their food arrived with little delay.

"This might be the best pizza I've eaten," he said ten minutes later, agreeing with her assessment. "Or maybe I'm just that hungry."

"I know what you mean. It's good, but you know, this could be anything," she said with a laugh. "I'm so hungry that..." She took a last bite of her slice.

"You forgot the end of your analogy," he reminded her.

"Literally," she said. "You're right. I have no idea what I was going to say."

They laughed. It was a relief to have that moment of lightness. So much had happened in such a short period of time. He could barely comprehend it himself. Few cases changed with the rapidity that this one had. It was an adrenaline rush that he hadn't expected.

It was dark by the time they left the restaurant and headed down a dead-end lane toward the inn they'd checked into. Some might have thought a shared room was not ideal but that was what he preferred.

He didn't want her out of his sight, not until he got her home and into the promised safe house and probably not even then.

"I'm so tired I could sleep leaning against a wall," she said with her usual humor but without the smile. "Trent? What is it? Why are you looking at me like that?"

"Your hair," he said as he stopped. They'd come around to the street in front of the hotel.

"My hair?"

"Yes. Damn, it was something we should have done earlier."

"There was no earlier, Trent. It's been the day from hell. I don't think we stopped for a minute except when we checked in, ate and now we're here."

"You're right but we need to do something now. It stands out,"

"I know," she said. "I thought of doing something myself." She looked at him and laughed. "Don't tell me you're going to give it a try?"

"You doubt me," he said with a laugh. "But yes, I am."

He looked at it, assessing what needed to be done. Her long blond hair was thick and hung straight to her waist. It was beautiful and that was part of the problem. Right now, she had it in one long braid. But even that wasn't enough. It was still too unique, too unforgettable.

She was silent, as if needing a moment to absorb that. "I thought I should color it at the least. And I was never sure if that was enough." Her voice shook.

"As it is, it definitely makes it a lot easier for you to be spotted," he said. He was pissed at himself for adding to her fear. But her hair was a key identifier and they both knew that.

"All right," she said as her eyes met his. "Get rid of it. Hair will always grow back. And color isn't forever."

"I'm sorry," he said.

"Don't be," she said and squeezed his hand. "Without you, I might not be standing here now. I'm in no position to worry about hair. And, besides, I knew myself that it needed to be done."

A block away from the inn, they crossed the street to a small market. Five minutes later, they were heading back to their room. He had a bag that contained a pair of scissors, hair dye, towels and a brush. He'd included the towels because the last thing he needed was to get dye on the inn's. For one, that was destruction of private property, but two, it would be evidence of what they'd done.

He glanced at her, saw the way she was puckering her bottom lip with her fingers. It was a nervous trait. He knew she wasn't happy with this, even though she'd thought of doing it herself and had admitted that. He admired her ability to compromise and do what was required. He guessed it was tough on her.

It took years to grow hair like hers. And it wasn't just the length, but the beautiful color that was as natural as everything else about her.

It was a messy process but an hour later it was finished. Tara's gorgeous locks were now mousy brown and styled in a blunt cut that squared off below her ears. The cut was amateur, and yet, while it didn't enhance her looks, it didn't take away from them either. He couldn't imagine any cut, any color, no matter how bad, doing anything to that. She was a classic beauty, and even without her iconic hair, that would still shine through. But they'd done what they could to make her less conspicuous.

"You've done this before," she teased him as she looked in the bathroom mirror. "You actually got it straight. Did you practice on your sisters?"

"No," he said. "They wouldn't let me touch their hair."

"But you knew exactly what you were doing so you must have done this before."

"Once," he admitted. And wished he hadn't. That case had almost had a tragic ending. Again, it had been the hair color that had made the difference. The woman had been able to slip under the wire. He never forgot that lesson, to consider even the most minor detail. It had been his first time in the field, and a close call. Things hadn't turned out well. And now he'd come close to doing it again.

"A bad end," she guessed. Her lip quivered as if she couldn't bear the thought. "She died. I'm so sorry."

"No, nothing like that. The witness is alive and well. She turned evidence. Turned out she was the guilty one," he said with a shake of his head.

A choked sound. Her arms clutched her elbows. He'd made her cry, damn it.

"I'm sorry," she said and wiped her eyes. "I was so prepared for you to say she died that I kind of heard that instead of what you actually said." She smiled and then laughed. And, he couldn't help himself, his laugh joined with hers.

"ARE YOU ALL RIGHT?" Trent asked as he came up behind her minutes later. He'd cleaned up the mess he'd made in the sink as he'd colored her hair and he'd cleaned up all the damning blond hair that was evidence of what they'd done.

Now he put his hands on her shoulders and she turned around. His dark blue eyes locked with hers. Their unchanging expression took her back to other times and other places. Only their separation had allowed her to forget for a time. There'd been other romances, other men and yet none had left a place in her heart like he had. Only one had come close: Mark. And even he hadn't been right. Worse, she hadn't broken it off when she should have, and it had ended in tragedy. It didn't make a girl lean toward romance.

"No," she said, pulling away from him.

"Tara?" He took a step closer. "Talk to me. I know what you went through was hell. I'm sorry you had to get caught up in…"

There was nothing to say. Much of it was inconceivable. What had happened, what could happen, even his being here. Her thoughts were mired in her emotion and she could explain none of it. Instead, she stopped him with a kiss. Her lips on his, the heat of them combined with a long-ago promise...

Her heart beat wildly as the kiss merely reminded her of what she'd never forgotten. It was a truth she'd feared facing. Her feelings for him had never died. They'd only changed. She was no longer the young girl with the runaway libido. And now it wasn't that she feared intimacy—she feared intimacy with him because it would bring back all those past feelings and then there would be no turning back.

She put her hands on his shoulders, meaning to step away when he claimed the kiss. He pulled her closer, his lips hot and full against hers. The kiss took her back in time and brought her forward. He'd been her first love. Gone were the wet, unskilled kisses of her youth. This kiss had only one thing in common with those: the heat.

"I never forgot," he said against her lips.

She pulled away from him. She needed distance before things went too far, pushing into a realm where they could never return.

"It was a long time ago," she said.

He looked at her as if considering everything about her. "You're still single. Why?"

She was surprised both that he asked the question and that he asked it in such a blunt way.

"I wondered," he said into her silent nonresponse. "That's all. I know that's an intrusive question. None of my business and—"

"Broken heart one too many times," she interrupted. "Maybe I'm a coward but I didn't want to ever lose someone I loved again. Three times," she said. "My father, my grandfather and Mark... He was a man I almost married," she said.

"Tell me about him," he said.

"He was my first serious romance. And I went out with him for too long. Long after I knew that he wasn't the man for me. The second time I came to San Miguel de Allende I was mourning him."

"Mourning?"

"He died in a traffic accident. He had an engagement ring in his pocket and our names were engraved on it." Her voice broke. "I'm sorry. I think the worst of it was that I didn't love him."

He took her in his arms and just held her while she sobbed. And it was then that she knew that the tears were those of guilt and regret. It was time to leave Mark behind. She pushed away from him and wiped her eyes with the back of her hand.

"I'm sorry. Grief goes away but it seems guilt hangs on."

He put his hands on her shoulders and looked deep into her eyes as she blinked back tears.

"I wish I could change the past," he said in a husky whisper.

"It's all right," she said in a whisper.

"No, it's not," he said and kissed her.

It was a kiss of comfort, at least that was what she thought she wanted. But in the end, it became a kiss of passion, of promises that lay unspoken between them and of a future that lay uncharted ahead.

Chapter Nineteen

The next morning, Trent woke up to a nagging sense of urgency. The little sleep he'd had was restless, disturbed by the slightest noise. His eyes roved through the dark room as if ferreting out any secrets that might be lurking, threatening her safety. He could hear Tara's soft, steady breathing telling him that she was still asleep. He looked at the old-fashioned clock radio on the nightstand. It was five o'clock. He flipped off the alarm so that Tara could have another few minutes of sleep.

They needed to hit the road and they needed to do it soon. Dark or not, in the next thirty minutes, they'd be coffee'd up, showered and on the road.

He slipped out of bed and went over to the coffee maker that was the only real amenity in the room. They'd needed a place to sleep and recharge, not luxury.

He'd been awake much of the night, listening to her every movement, hearing her mumbles and mutters as she fought a restless sleep. It was only when it sounded like she was crying in her sleep that he'd gotten up.

The sound of her crying had ripped at his heart and whether it was only a dream it didn't matter. He couldn't stand it. He had bridged the distance between them and took her in his arms. But holding her had been a mistake, for she'd been hot and soft in his arms, all the things he'd known she would be. He'd held her until she settled or, more aptly, for as long as he could stand to have her warm and supple in his arms. For as long as he could pretend that he wasn't affected, that it meant nothing.

When he'd returned to his bed, he'd lain on his back and stared at the ceiling. It seemed like he spent much of the night like that. He could have closed his eyes, but he'd known that it would make no difference. She was imprinted in his mind and, he feared, his heart. Holding her had only made it all so much worse.

He began to make coffee with the packets the hotel stocked the room with and added water from the bathroom sink. He never found this sort of coffee appetizing but right now he needed the caffeine jolt to face the day ahead. It was still early, too early, but they needed to get going.

With the coffee maker rumbling along, he took a quick shower. Five minutes later, he was dressed. The coffee was ready. He moved quietly over to the bed where Tara was still sleeping. He looked down at her. She looked so peaceful, her face beautiful as it was lit by the faint light that came from the back of the room.

He'd thought that the sound of the shower or the smell of coffee brewing might have woken her. Whether it was because she was exhausted or she was just a sound sleeper, she hadn't stirred. He'd let her sleep as long as he could. They couldn't waste any more time. They were still hours away from the border and even that didn't make them safe. They wouldn't be safe until he had her in a safe house where she couldn't be found. The fact that she'd been found once already—that there'd been a close call—was disturbing. The next time, they might not be so lucky.

"Tara," he said. His voice was soft. He didn't want to scare her or bring her out of sleep with a start. She'd had enough to deal with already. He wanted to make today better, make her feel safer.

"Tara," he repeated. He gently took her upper arm and gave her a little shake.

She mumbled and rolled over. In the muted light that spilled into the bedroom, her hair was a dull brown, so different from what it had once been. The cut was squared off, short and lifeless. He'd done her no favors there. But hair was hair, and like she'd said, it would grow back. A bad haircut or even a crappy color was nothing when compared with saving her life. That was what was important: keeping her alive.

"Tara," he said again, giving her another shake.

She opened her eyes. "Trent?" She sat up with

a start, rubbing one eye with the back of her hand. "What time is it?" she asked in a voice that had a bit of a grumble in it.

"Ten after five. We need to get going," he said.

"Of course." She pulled the covers back, revealing the T-shirt and shorts she'd slept in.

He handed her coffee in a cardboard cup. "Black, just the way you like it," he said.

She looked at him with surprise. "What did I do to deserve you?" she laughed as she swung her legs off the bed and sat up. The sound of her laughter was a relief against the night gloom that had yet to show hints of daybreak.

"Happened to be at the right place at the wrong time." What an idiot, he thought. Of all the stupid things to say, that was one of the worst. He was surprised when she laughed.

It wasn't a happy laugh. Instead it was abbreviated and dry.

"We've got about twenty minutes before we hit the road," he said.

"Time enough to shower," she said.

"Exactly," he replied as he made his way to the door to the room, closing it softly behind him. He needed to get away and get some air. He knew he couldn't be near the sound of running water because it would just stir up images of her naked beneath that water.

Outside, the air had a warm, muggy feel. It was going to be warmer than it usually got at the lake. The area was famous for year-round springtime temperatures. It was information he'd read in a pamphlet while waiting for the inn's manager to settle their bill. But the weather wasn't why they were here and the least of what he needed to consider.

What mattered was getting Tara out of here with no screwups. Time was tight.

The route Carlos had given him would take them along the back side of Guadalajara. The road would take them north without ever coming anywhere near the city limits. Trent trusted Carlos's information. The man had been in touch with a contact he'd claimed was at the federal level. Carlos hadn't named the contact, but it was his intel that had provided what routes were the best and quickest to get them north with the least trouble.

Getting confirmation of a solid, safe route had been a huge bonus. Tara had been through enough. The last thing she needed was more drama.

Carlos had painted an easy drive, a safe getaway. Trent hoped that it all turned out like that; from what he knew of the man, his connections were strong.

Trent jogged over to the twenty-four-hour convenience store and bought a disposable phone. Enrique needed to know about this delay.

"Sure enough. Safe trip, my friend," Enrique said before disconnecting.

When Trent returned to the room, Tara was ready to go. She was at the door, holding both their bags. "Ready to go." She smiled at him in a way that brought back other memories, memories from long ago.

He wondered what that smile cost her and appreciated the fact that she was trying valiantly to stay on an even keel, to pretend everything was normal. In a way, the smile brought him back to the girl he remembered as much as the woman he was just getting to know. They had one thing in common, the jokes they'd told and the joy she'd gotten from making the room at large smile. It was a joy he'd thought that he'd long since forgotten. They needed that talent now like he hadn't all those years before.

Except he couldn't think of one thing that might be funny enough to make either of them laugh.

"COME UP WITH the extra money or there's no deal. I'm not chasing her across the country. I've already got one man hurt and another on the line demanding more," Yago said.

"What do you mean?" Lucas asked, dread seeping into his belly. He had no control over Yago or the cartel that Yago belonged to. Instead, Lucas was stuck in the States and left to trust a brother he'd never trusted to do what needed to be done.

"Never mind. We had this conversation before. Ten g's aren't going to cut it. You need to double it. Otherwise, be prepared to face the little witch in the courtroom and kiss your little game goodbye," Yago said in a voice that held no emotion. "She'll be laughing in your face on trial day. But that's no surprise, is it, little bro?"

"Never mind," Lucas said, ignoring the gibes. Some things about their relationship would never change. "Get her. I'll have your money by the end of the week."

"You know what happens if you don't..."

The threat dropped but Lucas knew exactly what happened. There were people on both sides of the border who cared about nothing but money, or not even that. There were those who would do someone's dirty work because they owed favors. Or they were in it for the love of the kill. And his brother seemed to know them all.

Now there was no choice. Yago had to stop her. If his brother didn't, Lucas would go to jail. And if that happened, he'd never see the light of day again if they figured out what he'd done. He'd added one more murder to his list only yesterday when he'd killed Rico and his big mouth with a bat to his head. He hadn't thought. Instead, rage had taken over.

It was a complication he didn't need. But Rico had pushed him one too many times. He'd threatened Lucas's leadership of the States-based gang and shaken the rest of the gang's faith in him. It was time. Now Rico's body was buried in a ditch and his absence questioned by no one who wanted to live.

The pressure was on. Lucas needed the money, needed her dead to keep his freedom. Armed robberies spread thin was one thing. But stringing them together as he was doing was upping the chances of discovery.

But he had no choice. And it was all because of

that little witch. It had gotten to the point where what mattered most was the day the news arrived telling him she was dead.

Chapter Twenty

Trent looked in the rearview mirror. Lake Chapala was nothing but a speck of blue in the distance. At another time, he might have regretted leaving. It was a beautiful, calming place. If he'd had time, he would have explored each of the communities that called the lake home. He vowed that it would be a place he returned to under different circumstances. He couldn't help but appreciate the beauty of the large, still expanse of water.

They were heading north, taking the back way up and around Guadalajara. They would head to the town of Tala but they wouldn't stop. From there, they would angle their way farther north until they reached the border.

In the midst of these serious thoughts, his stomach rumbled.

"More breakfast?" Tara asked with a laugh.

He looked over as she dug into her bag. They'd been prepared for an early start and bought breakfast at a local convenience store last night. The choice of food had been grim if one was at all health conscious.

But it hadn't been the time to think about that; they'd needed quick and easy. Food in their bellies and coffee to keep them sharp. While the coffee hadn't set gourmet records, it had been strong. So far, they'd had bad hotel coffee and an extra strong cup from a specialty store on the outskirts of Lake Chapala.

The muffins she pulled out of her bag weren't much. But he'd take anything right now, including a slightly stale muffin purchased at a convenience store. He wondered if they should have bought more. While there were towns along the way, their next stop was hours away. He guessed they'd be living on packaged food until they hit the border and even beyond. Time was a precious commodity and they couldn't waste another minute.

Plus, they needed to stick to the back roads. Carlos had been adamant about that, telling Trent it would be the safest. In fact, he had a whole map from Tala onward in his head, courtesy of Carlos. Food was the last thing he needed to think about, he reminded himself. They wouldn't starve. They were talking days not weeks. Right now, he had more important things to consider. Getting the hell out of Mexico in one piece being the priority.

"Do you want to split the last one?" Tara asked.

He looked at her. She had a muffin in her hand and was peeling the paper from it.

"It's all yours," he said. "You finish it."

She shook her head. "Nope, mister, not going to happen." She broke the muffin in half and handed one half to him.

He smiled. She'd never been one to follow instructions well. He wasn't sure why she'd given him the option to refuse when acceptance was never her intent.

"It's yours," he insisted.

Dust drifted across the hood of the rental car. The road was paved but covered by the sandy soil of the fields that ran on either side.

His thoughts went from the road and back to Tara. She followed her own drum. She always had. That was fine back in Pueblo as kids, but here it was bloody dangerous. She'd already failed to follow his instruction more than once. Both times could have ended badly. First in the market with the gunman chasing her and then at her landlords' when she'd made a run for it. She'd been lucky, and if this were baseball—three strikes and you were out. The thought sent a chill running through him.

"Remember you used to always save me the last piece of any sweet?" she said with a smile.

He glanced at her and thoughts of wrongdoing fled. He'd do anything for her smile. "It's all yours," he repeated.

She shook her head. "No. We're grown-ups now. We share."

"As you wish," he said with a laugh.

"Milady," she replied, finishing off a phrase they'd used so many years ago.

He looked in the rearview mirror and could see a pickup truck coming up behind them. He dropped the muffin in his lap. He kept his attention on the road and on the mirror. He guessed that the truck had turned on from a side road. This was the first he'd seen of it. His attention went back to the road.

But a few minutes later, it was clear that the truck was intent on overtaking them. Nothing out of the norm, except for his gut, which was ringing alarm bells.

Tara looked over at him.

"Trent, what's wrong?" There was an edge to her voice as if she felt his tension.

He was concentrating on the road and on the truck that had halved the distance between them. Still, nothing wrong with that, and yet he felt uneasy.

"Is there a problem?" She turned to look behind them. "There's a truck behind us. It seems to be catching up."

"I'm not sure," he said. "It's the first traffic we've had behind us since we got on this road. That's not a problem, except they're coming on fast." He didn't say more. He didn't want her to worry in case he was wrong. Except he was never wrong about things like this. They needed to get rid of this truck, and instinct told him that they needed to do it soon. He put his foot on the gas, pushing the car five miles an hour faster, then ten.

The pickup truck was still gaining on them and sticking to the inside lane. The distance closed to a few yards. The truck should be getting ready to pass. It wasn't.

Tara turned around and let out an uncharacteristic swear word. "I think he's trying to run up our butt. Go faster."

His foot was heavy on the gas as they sped down the road. Still, he could see the face of the driver before the truck hit their bumper and sent them sailing ahead.

He choked back a curse as he slammed his foot hard on the accelerator, taking it to the floor.

But there was no escaping the truck. It was a bigger vehicle with a bigger engine and it sent them flying ahead on the road two more times. It would only be a matter of time before it sent them sailing into the ditch.

The truck rammed their back end again.

Tara screamed.

The rental car leaped forward as Trent fought to keep it on the road. The next time the truck clipped their bumper, it sent the car spinning. It was a fight to regain control, and they spun until they were in the other lane, facing the direction from which they'd come.

Trent did the only thing he could. He gunned the engine, taking the little vehicle to its limits and in the opposite direction of where they needed to go.

"Hang on!" he said, not even glancing at Tara. They needed to get out of the wide open, they needed people, a town and a place to disappear.

The pickup was coming up on his right-hand side. He veered. There was only one way out of this from what he could see.

"Get down!" he shouted. "Lean into me."

He slammed into the truck, forcing the driver to slow down, wrestling for control of his vehicle. He looked over and met the man's hard eyes. His face was swarthy brown, his dark eyes pinpoints of hate. But the surprising thing was how young he was.

Then the truck veered away and the face was gone. Trent had no choice but to turn his attention to the road, swerving to avoid the truck again. But there was only so much road and the truck slammed into them again.

Tara's head was down, both hands clinging to the seat.

One hit caught the truck at an odd angle. It was going so fast that it shot past them, sending them into another spin. Trent fought for control and when the car finally came to a stop, they were again facing north, toward Tala. Trent put his foot on the gas.

Tara twisted to look behind. "He's losing control. Oh my…he hit the ditch. And, oh…" Her voice trembled. "He rolled over. We've got a chance to get away from him, if nothing else."

He glanced in the rearview mirror. The truck was in the ditch exactly as she said, flipped on its roof. One front wheel still spun.

"You're sure you're all right?" he asked.

"Yes," she said. But a sheen of perspiration on her forehead seemed to say otherwise. It had been a crazy moment that could have had a very different outcome. The palms of his hands were still damp. They'd been lucky.

"Tara?"

"I'm all right," she repeated. "Really, I am." But her voice was just a whisper.

Guilt ran through him. This was his job. He expected such things. But he knew it was a nightmare for someone not in this line of work. This should never have happened.

"Damn it, Carlos!" He smacked the wheel. It was clear that this had been a setup. He didn't believe in coincidence, he never had. He'd trusted the wrong man. He'd taken information from the wrong source. He'd screwed up. This was completely on him.

They needed to get off this highway. His first thought was to head for the coast. From there, he had a number of options in their quest to go north.

They needed a new plan and a safe place to get it together. He sped down the road, heading to the next intersection. There was no way they were continuing along this route any longer than they had to. There was no doubt that it was compromised. How or why that had happened was something to consider later.

His first priority was to get off the route that Carlos had mapped.

As he thought that, there was an odd sound, like a clunk. Then the accelerator became heavy, almost unresponsive.

"What the hell?" he muttered. A feeling of dread snaked through him. He'd pushed it too hard and something had reached the breaking point.

"What's going on?" Tara asked.

"I don't know. It might be overheating. The engine

could be crapping out. Possibly gunning it the way I did…"

He didn't have time to finish the sentence before the engine died. He was able to coast it to the side of the road. Five minutes later, he shut the hood. There was nothing he could do. The only fortunate thing was that they'd put twenty miles between them and the pickup. The bad news was that they were still on the same highway, still easily found and much more vulnerable with neither wheels nor weapons.

He went to the trunk and grabbed a wrench. It wasn't perfect but at least he had something if somehow the occupant of that truck or someone else, were to come after them. Compiled with everything else, he wasn't going to take any chances. He tucked it into the back of his jeans and pulled his shirt over it.

"We'll get out of here, babe. No worries."

She stiffened. It was only then that he realized what he'd said.

Crap, he thought. The last time he'd called her babe, they'd been a couple of kids. It had slipped out, but latent feelings were the last thing they needed to deal with.

"Let's get going," he said, taking her arm as if he'd said nothing that might have offended her. "We've got to get off this road."

They had no means of communicating with anyone. They'd already dumped any electronics and he'd ditched the disposable phone he'd purchased earlier before leaving Chapala. The plan had been to get another one at the end of the day's drive. Now that plan was dead.

They had no map and no transport. The atlas had been left on the bus, forgotten. All they had was the route that Carlos had drafted for them. But that plan was compromised. And there was a good possibility that Carlos had set them up.

Trent wasn't sure what to believe. For now, he had to get Tara off this road and to safety. From here, he knew only the rough points, Guadalajara to the east, home to the north. West, that was the way they had to go. It was the only direction that hadn't been mapped out.

It was bad. A scenario like he'd never imagined.

Chapter Twenty-One

Trent couldn't believe this. They couldn't be more isolated. There was no sign of life either on the road or in the dust-blown fields that bracketed it. Not even a plane overhead. This wasn't worst-case scenario, but it was angling for a close second. In the distance the mountains rose into a telling blue sky. Ahead of them on the right was what seemed to be an endless field of blue agave. That told him that somewhere in this desolate stretch of road there was civilization. Somewhere.

"Trent! Where are you? I've been talking and…"

Not doing my job, he thought. "I'm sorry, my mind was elsewhere," he said. But he knew that if he'd done things differently, trusted differently, they wouldn't be in this mess.

"What do we do now? I don't know where we go from here and there hasn't been so much as a sign. Never mind that the atlas never came off the bus." She shook her head. "I'm sorry. I'm just stressed. I don't know…"

He put his arm over her shoulders. "Deep breath.

We'll get out of this and I'll get you home. I promise. Although…"

"What?"

"Nothing." He shook his head. There wasn't a hope of a ride was what he thought. There was no traffic. They had no choice but to keep walking. "We keep heading along this highway." He gestured to the pitted two-lane stretch of blacktop. "Until we come to an intersection that takes us west."

"Because the last thing you want to do is continue north."

"Exactly," he replied. "Too obvious."

The arm on her shoulder was only meant to reassure her. And yet, there was something about touching her, feeling her warmth, that turned him inside out. He needed her against him, needed to feel that she was alive and warm in his arms.

He pushed the thoughts away.

There was no one in sight. They were on an empty stretch of road, abandoning a broken-down vehicle, and none of that mattered. It was disconcerting. He could almost feel her fear as she looked up at him with a half smile and a nervous laugh.

"We'll get there," she said. "We always have before. We will now."

He wasn't sure what she alluded to, but it was all the invitation he needed, even though it was no invitation at all. He leaned down and kissed her.

Her lips were full and warm beneath his. She reached up, pulling herself closer to him. He could feel the warm pressure of her breasts against his chest, and feel the beat of her heart against his. He could taste the warmth and heat of her as his tongue danced against hers.

Time stopped before his brain finally kicked in. A long, blissful minute passed and then his logical voice signaled that here and now wasn't the place for a passionate embrace. He eased his hold on her, reluctant to let her go. His hands were on her shoulders, and the deep kiss ended. But he kissed her once again anyway. Not as passionately as before but more a celebration of being alive.

For a minute, they both stood there—the silent, dusty land sprawled out on either side of them. The road, an empty blacktop and the car sitting several yards back, a useless lump of steel. He'd been wasting time—lured by an attraction that was timeless. But that wouldn't solve their latest problem.

"I'm sorry," he said. "I shouldn't have."

"Damn you, Trent, don't you apologize," she said.

Except he had every need to apologize. What had happened shouldn't have, not here and not now. He'd wasted time that they didn't have. He'd felt safe in the fact that the truck couldn't be flipped out of the ditch and put back on the road, not with one man. They'd put enough distance between them, that was true.

But what was also true was that the driver more than likely had a phone and could call for a tow truck or more men. Men who would hunt them down.

They needed to get off this road, head in another direction and cover their tracks.

They walked for twenty minutes before they reached an intersection. The road was unpaved but, more important, it went west. There was no sign indicating what might be ahead. Cacti and dry desert stretched as far as he could see and all of it was cradled against a backdrop of distant mountains.

"I don't know where this goes but we need to get off this road," Trent said. "We don't have any choice but to take it."

And with that they turned west heading toward the unknown. Fifteen minutes later, they were tired and dusty and the small bottles of water that Tara had bought in Chapala were almost gone. There was nothing but chapped desert and desolation on either side of them.

But finally, there was a sign for a town ten miles away.

"Ten miles," she said with a sigh.

It seemed like forever and it would be hours till they got there.

The exhaust trail of a plane had Tara looking up.

"To think that we could be there, in luxury heading for home. Or at the least, economy class would feel like luxury," she said. "Imagine—miles dropping away every minute and us sitting there letting it happen. Maybe we'd have a drink, watch a movie." She looked at him with a smile. "I'd have a glass of red wine. How about you?"

He smiled, liking the diversion. "Right now, a cold beer—any kind, doesn't matter."

"You're right. I'm changing my order."

It was telling that their situation was so tough that economy travel seemed inviting. But right now that was the reality. A plane's cramped and perkless economy class would seem like luxury compared to this dusty road that had danger seeming to lurk at every corner.

Despite the fact that it wasn't as hot here as in other parts of the country, he was still sweating. They'd choked on dust and dread as the only car they saw sped by. That had been five minutes ago.

"It's quiet," Tara said and there was a nervous edge to her voice.

He took her hand. The gesture took him back. They'd held hands so often as teenagers. He'd left her in tears. He knew neither of them had forgotten but he wondered if she had ever forgiven him for what he'd said.

"Trent!"

Her shout had his attention. He turned, ready for action—to defend and protect. Her voice was high and shaken.

"Look!" She tugged at his arm as she waved with her other hand.

In the distance, a truck was just pulling onto the dusty road.

"Let's thumb a ride."

"What?"

"Hitchhike."

"Let me see what this is about," Trent said. "Don't forget the pickup. He could be coming after us yet."

"No, it's not like that." She shook her head. "Look at it. That truck is old and there's someone in the bed. Maybe two people or more, I can't see for sure."

"Let's not do anything rash," he said. "Let me—"

"And," she cut him off as if what she had to say next would clinch her argument, "looks like tools sticking out. Workers, I'd say. They're not out to get us. Besides, they turned off from the wrong direction. Nowhere near where we came from."

Her first point was valid; he wasn't so sure about her second. But the distance was quickly vanishing between them and he had to make a decision soon. His thumb ran over his back where the wrench was tucked into his pants. The truck was almost on them. Dust was billowing out from all sides.

It was now clear that she was right. It was more than likely a local farmer transporting goods or laborers from one place to the next.

"Trent!" Her voice had a command that dared him to refuse. She stuck out her thumb.

The truck pulled over. Hoes, shovels and rakes and an assortment of other tools were tied to the truck bed, where two teenage boys rode. There were three men in the front. All of it—men, boys and tools—was covered in dust.

"Hola," the man in the passenger seat shouted.

"Hola," Trent and Tara replied together.

The driver had sun-kissed, weathered skin and a friendly smile. The man in the middle mirrored the driver's smile. Neither of them looked threatening.

Trent relaxed slightly. There was no danger here.

"Ride?" asked the passenger nearest the window. His hair was pulled back in a ponytail. And his round face was dusty as if he'd already spent hours in a field.

"English?" Trent asked. He was keeping it simple. He couldn't be too careful and the last thing he needed was for them to realize that he was fluent in Spanish. Safe or not, people talked. And he didn't know where they were from or who they knew. His knowledge of Spanish, their appearance, every detail was information that could tag their identity. Most tourists weren't fluent in Spanish. Most weren't out here in rural Mexico. "Where are you going?"

A lanky kid in the back hung over the wooden slats. "To San Marie Antoine," he said in English that was only slightly less fractured than the passenger's.

Whether that was the next town or their final destination it was impossible to tell without reverting to Spanish and revealing what he could not. It didn't matter, the truck would get them farther than their feet would.

"Is there a bus from there?" Tara whispered to Trent.

His mind went over what he knew of the area from the old atlas and what he'd read later on the internet using the inn's computer. While this road hadn't been on the maps he'd looked at, the place the boy mentioned had.

"Yes," he said with a nod. He squeezed her hand and smiled at the look of relief on her face. If only it were all that simple, he thought. But they still had a long way to go to reach the border.

"Gracias," he said to the men in the truck. Those words were safe. Everyone knew them. He led Tara to the back of the truck and gave her a boost to help her up into the back. One of the boys gave Tara a hand, and with a jump and a pull, she was in. Trent followed.

It was another thirty miles to San Marie Antoine and the truck stopped five more times, picking up a total of six other people. Time dragged. But they were heading west and away from Guadalajara and the ill-fated town of Tala. And more important, away from the road that Carlos had them on.

Forty hot, dusty minutes later they hopped off the truck at the edge of San Marie Antoine. There was a gas station and, more important, a bus stop. He glanced at Tara. Her face was flushed and dusty. She looked tired.

"Okay?" he asked her as the truck drove off with a honk of its horn.

She waved before turning to him. On their left was the gas station and restaurant that also served as the bus station. They needed to go no farther. Everything was here, food and transportation.

"Hasn't been my best day," she said with a smile.

He was impressed with her resiliency. She'd been through hell the last twenty-four hours.

"You saved my life," she said. "Again." She took his hand and squeezed it. "I can't thank you enough."

He returned the squeeze. "I'll get you home, you can count on it."

"I know that now," she said.

Five minutes later, he had a sense that everything was falling into place. Just a few minutes ago, even the bus schedule had been promising. It was posted on the door of the small dusty building. The next bus would take them to the coast and was due in less than thirty minutes. Not only that but a connection would take them to a place he'd been before on another case. A known place was always a benefit, for it gave him a bit of an advantage. It was a bit of luck that he couldn't ignore. He looked at his watch.

"Let's get something to eat while we can," he said.

"That's an idea," Tara agreed. She reached for his hand and smiled as he looked at her with surprise. "A couple is much less suspicious than what we really are, don't you think?"

He wasn't sure what to say to that.

"Trent? I didn't mean that in a bad way. It's just—" she paused "—such a tough situation. We were something to each other way back as kids. But we've been living our adult lives apart. It's strange to be with you now."

"I suppose it is."

"That aside, I wouldn't want anyone but you protecting me, Trent. Just so you know," she said with a tremble in her voice. "Let's take this home."

Chapter Twenty-Two

"I never thought I'd crave a hamburger and fries in Mexico," Tara said with a small smile.

"I never thought it would be our only option," Trent replied. "Or that I'd ride in the back of a dusty truck with a bunch of Mexican farm workers."

Her smile widened. As she pushed her plate away.

The last bus had left an hour and a half ago and there was another arriving shortly. It would take them the first leg of their way to the coast. After that, they'd have a transfer and get to their destination, San Patricio, around dusk. The choice had been more chance than anything. They needed to go west and this was the first transport available.

With time to spare, they'd grabbed lunch in the tiny café that shared the space with a convenience-slash-souvenir store. The owner also sold bus tickets. A sign with the word *café* and an arrow pointed beyond a space crowded with chip racks, chocolate bars and magazines, a cooler with dairy and quick snacks, and a few rows of prepackaged foods, bread and cereal. Then there was an assortment of Mexican-themed souvenirs including T-shirts and caps. At the back of the store was what might be generously called a café. The only thing that separated the two spaces was a rack of pocketbooks on one side and a counter that held a dusty collection of ornaments and dolls. The break between the two displays formed a makeshift doorway. Beyond that was five small tables in a space that functioned as the café.

"Let's get going," Trent said.

They'd long since finished their meal and were now sitting at the table sipping waters as they waited for the bus, which should be here in the next ten minutes if it was on time. *Damn*, he thought. There was a good chance that it wasn't. This was rural Mexico and time took on a different meaning.

She walked ahead of him and his eyes kept being drawn to her hacked-off hair. Still, the smooth way she commanded a room hadn't changed. Tara had always had confidence. That was one of the many things he'd loved about her, one of the many things he admired.

Now she was picking her way around the close shelves of dusty tourist items. She had T-shirts in her hand. He guessed there was one for him. She'd already informed him that typical tourist souvenir shirts were perfect attire to fly under the radar. All he knew was that they were tacky. But she was right.

"Senor." The middle-aged manager came in and the screen door slammed behind him. "Senorita.

Your bus is coming. You have five minutes before it pulls in. You best get out there, he won't wait," he said in his slow, careful English. "He's already running late."

"Gracias," Tara replied as the manager rang up the check.

"Thank you," Trent said as he paid.

A minute later, she grabbed his hand as the bus pulled in.

It was a simple action and it meant everything. She'd trusted him from the beginning and he'd never break that trust. Unless she considered the fact that he'd bugged her. But he'd had a good reason and admitted what he'd done. She'd forgiven him for that. But now none of this was going as he'd expected. Despite that, he'd keep her safe. That was the one constant that he'd promised and the only constant he was determined to deliver.

TARA WAS EXHAUSTED. They'd been traveling for hours and had had to transfer buses once already. They'd gotten on the first bus shortly after lunch. Including stops at various communities and a transfer, the five-hour journey would stretch to seven. It would be evening before they arrived and then they would have to find a hotel.

The whole idea of it tired her. What had happened in the last twenty-four hours was draining. The few hours of sleep she'd had last night, combined with all that had happened today, had her fighting to stay awake.

She nodded off twice, at one point waking up with her head on Trent's shoulder. She'd apologized. But he'd interrupted her midapology with a chuckle and an invitation to use his shoulder anytime she felt like it.

She was drawn to him in ways that were too distracting for either of them. This was neither the time nor place. She guessed that it was only the situation that made her feel so close to him.

She told herself that, and yet she knew that it wasn't true. He did things to her, just as he had so many years ago when they had been a couple. Now the feelings were even more intense but the problem was they weren't a couple. He was here to protect her, to help. He was here for nothing else.

It wasn't the same for her. She couldn't forget. She'd tried over the years. She'd thought she'd forgotten him. And she had for a time, planned a life with Mark, but it hadn't been the same. She knew that now. If she were honest, she'd known that then. As if to confirm all that, she'd felt something much different when she saw Trent. And the kisses that they'd shared in the time that he'd been here had only reminded her of the desire that had always burned between them.

The longer she was with him, the more this became like a test of her willpower. The trip was taking forever as the bus pulled into one small community after another.

She glanced at Trent. He was on guard—watching everything. It was because of that she felt safe falling asleep. He was there keeping her safe, keeping them all safe. It was his job and it was what he'd always been good at even all those years ago.

The bus was crowded. They'd been lucky to get a seat. With each stop, more people got on. The close quarters combined with the heat and the lack of air-conditioning had many sleeping. She vowed to stay awake now; it was only fair to Trent.

She glanced across the aisle, where a man sat with a box containing two hens. He'd gotten on at the last stop. The smell of sweat and damp feathers was enough to make her sick. She wasn't sure who smelled worse, the hens or the man himself. She felt for the chickens trapped in the box. But it seemed the man did, too. He'd occasionally lower his head and speak in almost soothing tones to the birds.

"Don't tell me you have a thing for the chickens," Trent said. He'd been watching her. "I thought that look was just for me."

She looked at him, startled, and then realized he was teasing. She smiled. In a way it felt like old times.

And it was a relief to share a bit of humor, considering everything that had come before. Considering the unknown future. Humor would keep her sane, but it was Trent who had vowed he'd protect her.

She looked at him, at the strong jaw and the edge of a five o'clock shadow. And she wondered who was going to protect her from him.

Chapter Twenty-Three

San Patricio was a beautiful resort city that drew tourists from across the continent. It was smaller than many of the large communities that dotted the Mexican stretch of the Pacific Ocean and just big enough that they would go unnoticed. That was the reason that Trent had chosen it. From here, their route would be straight north, or as straight as he could go.

He needed to make a new plan. At this point, he wasn't sure whether they'd be driving, flying or, as a last resort, going by water. The only solid fact was that he was bringing Tara home. Or at least to the States and the safe house where they'd spend the next few months.

"Thank goodness," Tara said. Her face was pale and her new cut even rattier than before. The heat had done nothing for it. "I couldn't have ridden on that bus another minute. Too hot."

"You'd never survive living here," he said.

"Maybe not," she said.

They were near an area flush with accommodations of all sorts. There was no need to search for a hotel that met all their requirements: not too fancy, not too big, clean and accepted cash. He knew of one. It was a hotel where he'd stayed previously. From the hotel, they could even catch a glimpse of the edge of the Pacific Ocean.

"I'll get us registered," Trent said as they entered the worn lobby that smelled of disinfectant. A trio of umbrella plants took up the corner of the lobby and backed a couch and sofa. The tiles were a coppery color that was welcoming in the low lighting. To his right was the usual gathering of vending machines. The place looked all right. He could see no threat. It ticked all the boxes and it would do.

He'd used this hotel a few years back on a different case. His fake identification was still on file, just as it had been the year before that.

With the registration done and temporarily settled in another hotel room, doubts besieged him. Carlos had given them the route north on a little-used road, and on the very road he'd mapped, a truck had tried to run them off the road.

He'd thought about that as they'd traveled here, in the long monotonous hours as Tara had slept.

He remembered the conversation when he'd first met Tara's landlords, Francesca and Carlos.

"We have rooms available," Carlos said.

"Empty rooms because you refuse to advertise." Francesca looked at Carlos with a frown.

Carlos laid a hand on his wife's shoulder. "We've already talked about this, Frannie," he said with a tone of gentle resignation.

At the time, when Francesca had gently chastised

Carlos for not advertising, he'd wondered. As an ex-cop, Carlos hadn't been paid well. Yet, he'd been sure to tell them how he'd invested well and worked on the side. Why would he make a point of saying that? Was it because the opposite was true—that money was an issue? Yet he didn't seem driven to rent out more apartments and get more money. Did he not need the money? If he did, he could have received a kickback from the cartel to feed them wrong information. Or maybe he just had his sights on more money and loftier dreams. He'd seen lesser men corrupted by easy money no matter how dirty it was. Trent barely knew Carlos. And while Tara claimed he was a trusted acquaintance, the truth was that she'd stayed on his property a few times. He was a landlord, nothing more. It wasn't like they were old friends that he might feel any twinge of conscience about misleading them. Instead they were strangers he could misdirect for money.

Carlos more than likely knew nothing about the planned result of the deception. Trent guessed that he likely didn't know that his directions facilitated a murder plot. He wasn't sure why he was justifying the deception. But there was something about Carlos that made him want to doubt his guilt.

He pushed the speculation from his mind. What he needed to do was report this to Jackson. But first he needed to follow up with Enrique. They were too deep into Mexico and needed to get closer to the border. They either had to drive themselves or get in position for an extraction. Enrique was the expert on all of that.

After Trent lined that up, he would need to call

Jackson and let him know what was up and that they were fine. He also needed any updates from Jackson. Without intel, he was only guessing that they were safe at all.

First off, Trent purchased another disposable phone and called Enrique.

"I don't want to see you driving from there," Enrique said. "You were attacked going north but who knows what else has been leaked. I think the only safe thing to do is to fly you out. Stay low in the meantime."

They discussed what had happened. Enrique was adamant that Carlos would be charged with what he had done, and justice would be served.

"I'll have my man meet you in San Patricio," Enrique said. "He'll fly you from there up the coast. But it won't be until Tuesday."

"That's three days away. I don't like any of this, Enrique. I wanted to get her home as quickly as possible."

"I get that," Enrique replied. "But speed doesn't ensure safety. You know that. It's not just Tara whose life could be in jeopardy. You could endanger others with the wrong move. Despite what I said, I believe you're safe there. No one knows where she is. Let's do this right."

Trent agreed, and minutes later, he hung up. He put his next call in to Jackson and explained what had happened.

He gave Jackson the facts on how they'd been guided on their route by Carlos and then attacked. He listed his other doubts, beginning with the fact that the other rental units had been empty. The fact that Siobhan had mentioned how Carlos had turned renters away and yet he kept Siobhan on.

"I don't like the sounds of this," Jackson said. "Carlos recommends the route and then you're attacked. I'm not a fan of coincidence."

In the end, they agreed that the only thing that they knew for sure was that Carlos wasn't making the bulk of his living from his rental units or he would have been pursuing tenants, not refusing to advertise. Carlos's finances combined with his actions made him highly suspect and, as a result, untrustworthy.

"You went out on a limb on this one trusting Carlos as you did. And look where it got you. Stick to the known—Enrique. He's always been our go-to man."

Legally there are no financial benefits in a career as a cop in this country.

In hindsight, Carlos's words rang like an omen. Was it possible that he'd been on the take and Trent and Tara had been delivered into the hands of men paid to take them out? If that was the case, fortunately, they'd escaped.

"Yeah, I got it, Jack."

"Now, as far as getting you home. We'll use Enrique's plan. He's there and he knows Mexico intimately, not something I can claim."

A minute later, Trent hung up. What he'd gotten from both the calls was that for the next three days, he and Tara were on their own.

Chapter Twenty-Four

"There's no proof," Tara said with her hand on Trent's arm after hearing the new plan and the doubt cast on Carlos. "I don't think Carlos is guilty of purposely giving us information to put us in harm's way."

"I don't know. What Carlos said was pretty damning," Trent said. "Like I said, he gave us the exact route and that was where we were attacked."

"I hate to believe it. I saw no evidence that he was dirty at all. That he was getting money from criminals." Tara shook her head. "No, I don't believe it."

He agreed with her to a point and yet he was reluctant to side with her. This would play out as it would no matter what either of them thought.

They talked as they walked along the shore. It was early evening and he'd remembered that only a block away from their hotel was a small restaurant that specialized in barbecue steak. Five minutes later, they had a table.

She looked at him with a smile. "Two meals in a row that remind you of home. And I thought you were a traveler."

"I am but not by choice," he said. "For a time, I went overseas. My assignments took me there."

"Paris, South Africa?" she guessed dreamily.

"Neither one," he said. "Lately my assignments have been closer to home."

"Mexico with me," she said with a laugh.

He looked at her and was overwhelmed by the sense of wanting to know everything about her, everything that he had missed in the years they'd been apart.

Whoa there, he thought. *You're on a fast track to nowhere.* But he'd known from the moment he'd taken this case that he'd done so because he wanted another chance to make her his.

"So, anyone special in your life?" she asked. "Did you ever marry, have kids?"

"No kids but I was engaged once," he said.

"What happened?" There was a strain in her voice as if she thought every relationship ended in tragedy.

"We weren't right for each other," he replied. "She liked the rush of what I did for a living more than she liked who I really was as a person. And," he added looking at her, "I'd already lost my heart a long time ago to someone else."

Tara said nothing. But it was clear that she was uncomfortable. Instead of looking at him, instead of replying, she looked away.

Damn it, Nielsen, he said to himself. Wrong time, wrong place.

A street hawker motioned to them through the

window to look at the tray of dolls that hung from his neck.

"Trent, you have nieces. Let's go take a look."

Her voice had a forced happiness to it.

Some things didn't change. She still had that knack for making him talk about his personal life. During their long bus ride, she'd asked him about each of his sisters, forgetting not a name nor an age, and she'd wormed out of him the fact that he was an uncle courtesy of his oldest sister. She seemed to take joy in talking about his siblings. Maybe, he thought, because she had none.

Now she grabbed his hand and dragged him outside, where he waited while she examined the porcelain dolls dressed in vibrant red, green and orange costumes. They were small, easy to transport and in the end, she convinced him to purchase two of the dolls, one for each of his twin nieces. The girls were only two and he guessed that his sister would appreciate the gesture more than the twins would enjoy the dolls.

"Here," Tara said. "Give them to me. They're small enough to fit in my bag." She'd bought a bag with the same vivid design as the dolls only fifteen minutes earlier. Or more accurate, Trent had bought it for her.

They slipped back into the restaurant. Their absence seemed to have gone unnoticed amid the laughter and music. A quartet of men and women dressed in white shirts with either red pants or skirts danced to the music of a guitarist and an accordion player.

The music was more amateur than professional, but the enthusiasm made up for any lack of skill.

"Strangest steak house I've ever been in," Tara said with a giggle.

The light laugh was music to Trent's ears. He enjoyed watching her as she laughed at the antics of a girl who got up and tried to dance with the band. And she clapped as loud as the others when it was over.

They ordered steak, and margaritas were brought to their table. Trent had ordered his usual virgin drink. He had a hard rule: no alcohol of any kind while on assignment. For Tara, he didn't think it would do any harm. There was no danger around, but it was his responsibility to make sure of that, not hers.

"So, there's someone in your life now?" he asked. There wasn't, not that he knew of. But he wanted to make sure. He'd lost his heart to her once, although his treatment of her at the time would illustrate otherwise. He'd been a typical teenage boy, projecting his hurt onto someone else.

She shook her head. "No. You?"

"No."

Their steaks arrived and for a few minutes they ate in silence.

"I feel silly saying this," he said.

She looked up, her fork in one hand and concern in her beautiful eyes.

What the hell, he thought. He needed to get this off his chest.

"Say it," she encouraged.

"It was a long time ago, Tara, but I always wanted to say I was sorry for the way we broke up. I said there was someone else but there was no one. It was just a boy's hurt feelings. It wasn't like you had a choice. Your family was moving, you had to go. But I blamed you and acted like a jerk because of it. We could have kept in touch. We could have seen each other even, just not as often. Instead I broke it off."

"Trent, like you said, it was a long time ago."

"Don't, Tara, I need this. I need to apologize." He put down his utensils. "It sounds silly to speak of it now but it's part of who we are and what I'm trying to say is that I'd like—"

"Trent, are you saying you'd like to date me?"

"I'm saying that I never forgot you and I'd like another chance. The grown-up version."

"Trent, no, I—"

"Tell me you're not attracted to me." If there was one thing he was, it was persistent, a result of being the only boy in his family. His father had died years ago. That had left him, his mother and three sisters. Persistence had occasionally trumped being outnumbered and often outvoted.

She looked up. "Don't make me say it," she said in a soft voice.

"Say what?"

"I never forgot you and I never wanted to let you go in the first place. There, I said it." She stood up. "Pay the bill. I'll be outside."

Five minutes later, he found her. Her back was to him and she was standing on the edge of the boardwalk that fronted this block of restaurants. She turned as he approached.

He took her hand. "Like I said, I never forgot you either, Tara."

They walked back to the hotel in silence. But at the door to their room, she turned to face him.

"This doesn't mean what you think it does," she said.

"Excuse me?"

"Sex isn't even on the table." Despite what she'd said, she stood on tiptoe and kissed him. Her hands slid down his chest and her body followed and made him feel every curve. "I'm just warning you. If we go there, I don't know if I can turn back."

He knew what she meant. There was too much history between them already, sex took it to another level.

He looked at her with fresh appreciation and was reminded of another of the many things he'd loved about her. There were never any games, she told him exactly where he stood and what to expect.

He closed the hotel room door behind them.

"Let's start this right," he said and tried to keep his expectations low. He'd be happy with whatever outcome she decided on. He kissed her, her lips hot and soft beneath his. Her body pressed against his. The softness of her, the small moan that she shared as his tongue touched hers, as his hands moved lower, were erotic. It was like the past had come alive and yet this was nothing like the past. That had been hot, but this took it to another level.

"Trent, no. Stop, please."

She spoke in midkiss, making the words like caresses against his lips.

"Stop."

It took seconds for that word to register in his passion-dulled brain. He was thankful that she'd put a stop to it both in her earlier words and now her actions. There was no way he could have. He was caught in the moment.

He let her go and went to the washroom, where he rinsed his face and hair, as if the cool water would also cool his desire. When he came back, she was sitting on the edge of the bed. He sat down beside her.

"I keep forgetting that you have a whole other world that you'll return to after this is over, a job that's a world away from what I do." She shook her head. "I'm going to miss this." She paused. "You."

He took her hands. "Right now, you are my job. But you're so much more than that."

"Trent, don't." She shook her head. "There's so much you don't know about me."

"Like what?" He waited, wondering what it might be. He was sure that he knew pretty much everything about her. Or at least, he thought he did. He'd known her years ago and he knew her now. There were no secret children or husbands squirreled away. That would have been dug up. It would have been part of her file. That was necessary information.

"I loved and lost," she said sadly. "Or more accurately, I was loved and lost."

"We were young and I was stupid."

"It wasn't you," she replied. "You get over that young love…"

Despite her earlier claim, that was a slam to his ego. It was harsh and unlike her. He wondered where that had come from. As he thought that, the hope that they could rekindle their relationship slipped away. She didn't feel the way he did. He'd seen the signs all wrong.

"I'm sorry," she said. "I didn't mean it quite like that. It's just that my last boyfriend, Mark… The way he died devastated me." She looked up with teary eyes. "The guilt of knowing that he died thinking that I loved him, that I'd marry him, almost killed me."

"Ah, Tara. I'm so sorry." Trent took her in his arms and held her. "But he died believing you loved him. That's not a bad thing."

"I know that now," she said. "Thank you."

"You're welcome," he said with a bemused smile at the direction the conversation had gone.

"We should call it a night," she said.

Fifteen minutes later, she had washed up and tucked herself into the far edge of the bed. It was like she was a ball field away. She yawned, pulling the covers to her chin. But her gaze was on him.

He sat on his side and pulled his shirt over his head.

"What happened?" she asked with a frown.

He knew what she meant. It was hard to miss the scar that had almost killed him. The thick eight-inch scar that ran down his right shoulder.

"I took a knife during a drug bust," he said.

"You could have been killed! Trent—why? Why do you do this?"

"Because someone has to do it and—"

Her fingers were soft on his skin, hot and tingly as they ran down the scar. He couldn't say anything or, more accurately, didn't want to say anything. The scar said it all and her touch made him melt. If silence brought more of such caresses, he could be silent forever.

"You always wanted to do this, be in law enforcement. I remember you talking about it. I'm so proud of you, Trent. And I'm sorry. I shouldn't have questioned your motives. I know why you do it—it's your life."

"It's a job," he said, brushing away her praise as something he had no need for. He needed her in other ways.

He leaned forward, the erotic feel of her touch gone. She'd said those words about being proud of him like she was some sort of mother figure. She'd never been that to him and she never would. She was his first love.

"It's who you are." She sat up, the oversize T-shirt sagging around her but failing to hide her curves.

He tore his gaze away from the beauty that was off-limits to him, and instead looked at her face, her dark expressive eyes.

"What do you mean?" he asked.

"You accomplished a dream," she said. "To be in law enforcement. I remember when you first told me but even back then that was old news. It's in your blood. In fact, I remember your mother saying that. How is she?"

"Making her own life and doting on her grandkids. She's living in a condo and doing some traveling," he said. "And you're dodging the question. What do you mean, it's in my blood?"

"Your triple-or-so great-granddad was a cop in London. I'm not sure how many *great*s were attached to that." She looked at him and laughed. "Don't look so surprised."

"When did my mother tell you that?" he asked. The annoyance was replaced with a bit of pleasure that she had cared enough to remember such a trivial fact.

"Years ago," she said. "I was in high school and still in Pueblo. Obviously," she added the last almost as an afterthought.

"And you didn't forget," he said. He remembered her penchant for history—world, personal, other people's families, all of it.

They were quiet for a minute or two.

"Good night, Trent," she said as she turned out her light.

He thought she'd fallen asleep until she spoke again.

"I don't like putting you in danger," she said.

"Get some sleep."

Ten minutes went by. He stared at the ceiling. She lay on her side but kept twisting and turning. Finally, she sat up.

"I can't sleep," she said. "And it looks as if you can't either."

He got up and came over to sit down on the edge of the bed, his arm around her. He massaged her shoulders. "Stop thinking or you'll never sleep."

"You should talk," she said with a laugh that took the edge off the words. "Why don't you snuggle next to me, instead of the distance of Madison Square Garden away?" She looked at him. "Don't look like that, Trent."

"What do you mean? You can't see in the dark."

"I can see everything about you, Trent Nielsen. Okay, I can sense. And what you're thinking is not what I meant. Nothing like that. Just some old-fashioned cuddling might calm us both down."

"Maybe," he said and knew that she was more wrong than she'd ever been in her life. He only hoped that she fell asleep fast.

He lay down beside her and turned her face to his, giving her a gentle kiss. She pulled back.

"Don't," she said as she put a finger to his lips and then her hands were on his shoulders as she kissed him. "Just hold me," she whispered, her lips brushing his.

But the heat of her body, its softness and the words that were like a promise between them had him hard without a conscious thought. He twisted his body slightly away from her so that she'd never know what she'd done or what his body demanded.

She lay with her head on his shoulder and his arm across her belly. It was a belly that was firm, as if she worked out. He'd noticed that before and he'd said nothing. Her breathing was regular, as if just having him near had relaxed her enough to sleep. He'd hoped when she'd asked to cuddle that she meant more, that the feel of him beside her would have her wanting him. He should have known better. She was stronger than that. He knew that now. She'd run from death once again and only the pallor in her face earlier or her trouble sleeping gave any indication of what she'd escaped.

Within minutes, he could hear her steady breathing, knew she slept.

He lay thinking of tomorrow and the next few days, how they'd spend the time until Enrique got them out of here. And it was heading toward the wee hours before he finally dropped off for a few hours of sleep. His thoughts had been plagued with the fact that she'd run from death and she'd survived— twice. By the law of averages, her luck had run out.

It was up to him to change Lady Luck.

Chapter Twenty-Five

The morning sun was bright. Trent squinted as he looked down the street. He was standing just outside the hotel. He'd made it to the lobby by the stairs in record time. He'd left his sunglasses in the room in his haste to find Tara.

He couldn't believe she'd just disappeared, couldn't believe after everything that had happened that she'd do this. She'd been gone when he'd gotten out of the shower.

He was angry and sick with worry at the same time. Surely she knew the danger in going out alone. They might be in a place that he thought was safe. But there were no guarantees. There was always the wild card. They could never take the chance.

What the hell was she thinking? They'd done this before. She knew the routine. She'd seen what could happen, the possibility of danger exploding around them. He stood on the sidewalk just outside the hotel and tried not to fume. Where was she?

He scanned the street. It was empty, too early in

the morning for many to be out and about. He heard a car door slam. Someone called out a window. And then there was silence.

"Trent."

He spun around.

She had just come out of the hotel and she looked rather sheepish. "Were you looking for me? You didn't think..." Her hand was on his arm. "I was just admiring the art on the wall in the small room adjacent to the lobby."

Relief flooded him at the sight of her. "You scared the crap out of me," he said. "Don't do that again. Promise me."

"I promise, Trent." She looked at him and put a hand on his arm. "I'm sorry. I really frightened you, didn't I?"

"I was afraid that some harm had come to you. I couldn't bear if—"

"Don't say it," she cut in. She looked at him in a way that made him melt. She seemed unaffected, like she had a core of steel, and yet she was turning him into a melting pot of desire.

"Let's get some breakfast," he said. It was better to think of other things. "And please, don't slip away like that again. Anything could happen. We don't know who could be on the streets. No matter how careful I am, there's always a chance..."

"That someone is here looking for me?"

"Exactly," he said. "Remote possibility but one that should never be discounted."

TRENT CHECKED IN with Jackson later that day.

"I've spoken to Enrique," Jackson said. "There's a small runway outside of town. Do you know it?"

"I do." Trent had mapped out the area on the hotel computer on arrival.

"You're still on. Meet his man there, like he said, at 6:00 a.m. Tuesday morning," Jackson went on, giving other details.

Trent hung up feeling relieved to finally see a window to getting Tara out of here and home to safety.

THE DAY WENT by as if they were typical tourists. They strolled the beach, checked out the shops and enjoyed the sun.

But the dangers weren't over. There was still the danger of the night. They'd shared a room before, last night and the night before that. But sharing a room with her wasn't getting any easier. If it had been just a room, he might survive, but the bed was going to kill him.

The thought of her so close, hearing her move softly in the night, sensing her presence, it was all pushing the limits of his restraint. No matter what he told himself, he was still tempted. So far, he'd made it through without stepping over the boundaries he set for himself. He'd never felt this way about another woman but with Tara it was different. With the second night looming, with a king-size bed and nothing but inches between them, he wasn't sure if his willpower would hold. He was thankful he had her iron will to rely on, for she'd already dictated no sex.

"It's been a long day," he said, tossing the bed dilemma out for now. "Let's grab something to eat and call it an early night?"

"I'm not hungry," she said and there was a strange expression on her face. One he'd never seen before. "Not for food."

He stood there for a moment, hearing what she'd said but not translating it, not immediately.

"Trent," she murmured, and she put her arms around his neck and kissed him.

The kiss was hot, long and passionate. It promised other things and was all the invitation he needed. He wanted her in every way a man wants a woman. He wanted her in his bed and he wanted to make her his, to be hers. There was nothing about her that he didn't want.

He had to end the kiss and he couldn't, for the kiss was passionate, her lips heavy on his. The heat of her pressed against him and her body, all of it too tempting to let go. Especially when he had to be the one to stop it.

"I know what I said last night. But I was wrong. I never forgot you, Trent. No one else could compare." She said the words against his lips. Her breath hot against him, just like everything else about her.

At first he felt, more than heard her words. What she said didn't register right away. When they did, they were words he'd never thought he'd hear. She'd been lost to him. But she'd never been forgotten.

He wondered why she was saying these things to him now after all these years. Did she mean them, had she, like him, never forgotten what they once shared? Or, when he delivered her home safe, would it be over?

"It was so long ago," he said against the softness of her too-short hair. "And I never forgot you either." He wasn't sure why he said that, for now he was playing her game and he wasn't so sure that he was going to come out unscathed.

"Kiss me," she breathed, as if that wasn't exactly what he'd been doing.

But his thoughts were blown away as her full lips opened and gave him the chance to take the kiss to the next level. Reason was gone as he explored the hot passion of her and was promised so much more.

He couldn't do it.

He pulled away, letting her go. Someone had to insert sanity into this situation. Their relationship was destined to go nowhere. Each of them had their own life. And this was just a moment of insanity in a crazy race to save her life. She was acting out of character and he wouldn't take advantage of the situation, as difficult as that might be for him. She was his priority.

"Tara. This can go nowhere."

"Nowhere is all we need," she said. "We've got tonight."

He didn't know what that meant. He didn't have the will to even process the words. His brain seemed to have taken a siesta. With her body pressed against him and the passion offered in her eyes, he had no more direction than a rag doll. Her touch brought back every desire he'd never forgotten. He was in hell, and he was in heaven. She'd opened the gates wide when she stood on tiptoe, when her body ran down his as she sank back down to the flat of her feet. He was beyond aroused and soon there'd be no going back.

"Trent."

He had to drive the passion from his mind. He had to take control of the situation or this would head to nowhere good.

She tasted of cinnamon. He remembered the stick of gum the man with the chickens had offered her on the bus. She'd put it in her pocket, for later she'd said as the man had smiled and told her how the chickens were going home to provide eggs for his family. They'd even had names.

Chickens.

Damn it to hell, Trent. You're thinking of chickens when... It was that or succumb.

Succumb to what, what the hell was he doing? He was a train wreck.

She was on tiptoe again. Her body touching his was like an erotic caress. Her fingers followed her body and there was no stepping away from this.

"Tara..." Still he tried to stop it, tried to be in charge of his desire, his body—something. He really did. He knew what needed to be done. He even told himself that he wanted to take a step back.

Her tongue caressed his bottom lip, her hands

behind his head, pulling him down toward the bed. The soft heat of her was too tempting and he struggled with his desire. It had been too long. His memories of her too rich and the reality so much better than the fantasies. Still he resisted that last fall to the bed.

"Make love to me, Trent."

At the words, his throat felt as tight as other parts of his anatomy. Yet some small part of him didn't want this to happen now, not like this. That he would finally make love to her here in a faded hotel room, in a country that wasn't their home, didn't seem right.

"Tara…" It seemed that was all he was capable of doing, repeating her name. He wanted her like he'd never wanted a woman in his life. He wanted her but, more important, he needed her. And he didn't know where they stood on either of those things. It didn't matter, for he was floundering in the heat of passion.

"Remember when we were kids? Remember the first time we made out?" She chuckled. There was little mirth but something was almost hot in the way her eyes met his.

He cupped her face in his hands. "I wanted our first time to be special."

"It was," she said as her hands slid under his T-shirt. "This is now."

That wasn't true, not really. Back then, they'd only gone partway. But memories of the past vanished as her fingers danced across his skin and her mouth followed her hands.

"Tara…"

She looked at him with a smile that was all woman. She knew what she was about. And she was going to get what she wanted. What they both wanted.

This was outrageous, he had to take charge. And as he thought that, the zipper of his jeans was down. His jeans slipped over his hips and her hands went to new places, places where she led the show and he could never turn back.

Her hands were hot. They burned his skin with a heat that he craved. He had to at least slow her if he couldn't stop her. Neither of them had the willpower for that. But if they didn't slow down, he'd lose it right now. It would be a quick end to a passionate beginning.

This was the moment he'd dreamed of all those years ago. He wasn't going to lose it in a passionate moment that shot off like fireworks at the Fourth of July in a show that lasted under a minute. No, he'd give her better than that.

He kissed her. Her lips were hot on his. Her body pressed against his like it was made for him. He knew if they did this, if he made love to her, that he couldn't walk away. For the first time in his life, he could say out loud that he loved her. Except out loud was a commitment. Sex wasn't. At least it never had been. He wasn't ready… But with this woman everything was different. Sex was only about pleasure until now. Now sex was a commitment, a promise, and for him the deal was sealed.

"Trent?"

There was no denying what they both wanted. He let her lead, let her take them down to the bed. She was half in his lap, half off. He shifted her, moving her a little farther away so that he could more easily slip his hands under her T-shirt. His fingers caressed her smooth skin, skimming it in a teasing manner as he slipped the shirt over her head. Her bra followed.

His hands and lips were soon offering sensations of their own. The sounds of pleasure she made in the back of her throat, the way she arched toward him as if asking for more, only turned him on more. His lips and his tongue gave her what she wanted as he slipped her jeans and panties off. Soon, the rest of his clothes followed.

Her hand brushed his jaw. Her breasts were soft and yet firm against his chest and her touch along his upper arm was erotic. He couldn't have stopped his reaction if he wanted to. He wanted her. When she arched her body into his, it was a promise that lay like a gift between them. She was hot in his arms.

It was no longer she that needed saving, but him.

Her hands were on his shoulders, and she was drawing herself as close and tight as she could. Her breath was sweet, the heat of her lips molten against his neck.

"Trent." She seemed to breathe his name.

She was unstoppable. Passion held him captive. Her hands on his skin were a caress that was red-hot with promise. There was magic in her touch.

She was on top of him. In a way, he liked following her lead. There was something erotic about it.

He ran a finger along the satin heat of her skin. He dipped his hand down to her trim waist and past, feeling her wet and ready.

"Tara."

"Now," she commanded. "It's been long enough."

It was her hand that finally guided him. She who finally ended the erotic torment and gave them both what they craved. They sailed to the heavens and back. And they did it again, as if once would never be enough.

Later, they lay spooned together. Hunger was what finally separated them. They got up, dressed and went out into the hallway to forage from the vending machines. Then they sat with bags of chips and chocolates around them, laughing like kids as they shared the various packages. They made love again, and it was only sometime after midnight that they got any sleep at all.

At least, she slept. He lay there looking at her and thinking that this was a night that he'd never forget. This was the woman he'd always loved, and this time he wasn't going to let her go.

Chapter Twenty-Six

Early the next morning found Trent and Tara walking to a café for an early breakfast. They'd had little sleep. She'd been awake at daybreak and he'd barely slept all night. Holding her in his arms had been so new and he hadn't wanted to miss a moment. He'd held her as she'd dreamed through the night and kissed her when she'd awoken numerous times. It was in those times when her caresses had teased him that they'd made love twice more. The dawn had come too early. But every moment that he hadn't slept had been worth it. They'd lain there for a long time, quiet, just enjoying each other. And finally, shortly before seven, they'd gotten up and showered.

"Aching for that first cup of coffee?" he asked.

She looked up at him with a smile. "Amazingly, no. I'm more hungry than anything."

"Really? I'm not sure if I believe that," he teased. That was something he'd learned about Tara. She wasn't shy about food or her appetite. That was different from the girl he had known and something he'd quickly learned about the woman she'd become.

"Believe it," she said and smiled at him. Her stomach grumbled. "See? All that junk food only kind of took the edge off."

He smiled at her and took her hand.

"I can't believe how quiet it is," she said. "I know now that if you want a seat in a restaurant, seven in the morning will do it. Provided they're open," she said with a grin. "Everyone must be still getting their beauty rest."

He squeezed her hand, leaned over and gave her a kiss.

"Look at this, Trent," Tara said as she leaned away from him to look at a shop window.

It was the last moment of peace before chaos erupted.

It was barely a crack of air, there and then gone. But the shot that was fired at them sent him spinning around as the bullet lodged in his right arm. The force of it drove him against Tara, and he wrapped his left arm around her, taking her to the cement sidewalk. He took the brunt of the fall with a grunt.

"Trent!" she screamed. She rolled off him instantly, as if realizing that he'd been hit.

He stood up immediately. He knew there was no time to determine injuries. His right arm burned with a heat that he'd only felt once before. That time, it had been a knife that had slashed across his back. But this time, the pain wasn't that bad. Not yet. He couldn't think about that, about pain. He only knew they had to get the hell out of here.

"There." He pointed to a space between buildings.

"Go now," he demanded. He could smell blood. His blood.

"Trent!" There were tears and panic in her voice.

"Damn it, Tara. Take cover." He gave her a little push. "Go!"

She looked with shock at the blood that ran between his fingers. And then she turned with a nod and ran between the two buildings. He blew out a sigh of relief, even as pain hit and rocketed through him.

He turned and scanned the street for their attacker, but there was no one. It was like the shooter had disappeared or never been there at all. The silence was almost unnerving.

"Son of a…" He bit off the expletive. He vowed that the scuzzball wasn't going to get away with this.

He glanced back. Tara was just behind him, still between the buildings. Her head was peeking around the corner, watching. The look on her face said that she was poised to help.

He waved at her to stay.

She nodded.

He made his way up the street, keeping close to the buildings. He paused twice, clenching his teeth against the pain. But there was no sign of the gunman. A minute passed, then two. Then he saw him. The back of a thin, dark-haired man running, heading for a parking lot, a gun in his hand.

"Damn it!"

He was getting away.

Trent ran after him, keeping to the inside of the

sidewalk, as if keeping close to the buildings would keep him hidden from view. The man turned around, saw him and shot. This time he missed. But Trent dropped to the ground, giving the illusion of being hit. The sudden movement almost killed him, the pain sharp and brutally intense as it ripped down his arm.

The man turned and walked away at a fast clip, as if he thought Trent was no longer a threat.

Trent followed. He was at the corner of the last building on the block and across from him was the parking lot. The shooter was only twenty-five feet away. The piece of slime thought Trent was down and he'd turned away, intent on his own escape.

Trent gritted his teeth, got to his feet and powered into a run, pushing himself to hit top speed. The man turned but already it was too late.

Trent tackled him one-armed, throwing him face-first to the pavement. The gun flew out of the man's hands and clattered across the parking lot.

He couldn't hold him. His left arm wasn't enough. And his right arm had pain knifing through him like someone had taken a lighter and set it on fire.

The man yanked himself from his hold. He leaped up and ran, heading across the parking lot.

A shot rang out from behind and the man stumbled and fell.

"What the…" Trent rose up in a sitting position using his good arm and turned to see what had happened.

Tara was standing there holding a gun.

"Where did you get that?" he asked as he stood up.

"You mean thank you for saving your life?" she asked. But her hand shook even as she said the words.

"Where did you get that?" he repeated. All his yearnings to have a weapon in his hand, to be able to carry again ran through the question. And there she was with a gun, calmly standing there as if she did this every day. The irony didn't escape him.

"It's his," she said. "When you tackled him, the Ruger went flying."

He noticed she called the gun by its make. And remembered her grandfather's formidable collection.

"I never liked guns," she said. "Now I'm grateful I have one in my hand."

"You and me both," he said. Movement caught his eye. A police car. It was a block away and had just turned onto a street that intersected the parking lot and then turned again, away from them. For now.

A new urgency ran through him. She couldn't be seen with a weapon. As a foreigner, a gun in her possession would have her thrown in jail indefinitely.

"Give it to me," he said.

She handed it over. "Gladly." Her hand shook. He guessed it was a result of the aftermath. Her shot had been too accurate for anything but a steady hand.

He wiped the gun with his T-shirt and then quickly pitched it into a garbage bin on the street. He reached in and yanked out newspapers, burying the weapon.

"Thank you," he said to her, taking her hand with his left. "But don't ever do that again."

"I hope I never have to," she said with a tremble in her voice. "But I won't ever be afraid to pick one up in a pinch. That was both frightening and exhilarating."

The police car had returned and was moving slowly down the street as if they suspected something.

"Let's go," he said with an attempt at a smile. "And get out of here." He glanced over at where the police had stopped. He let go of her hand and pushed her forward with one hand. They needed to move quickly but not quickly enough to garner attention.

He glanced behind them and saw the shooter struggling to run the last few feet that would have gotten him out of the parking lot. But Tara had wounded him. He heard the shout of an order from the police. Then a shot rang out and the man fell again.

They needed to get out of here before the police realized their involvement in the situation.

"Oh my." Tara clenched her fists. Her fingers were shaking.

"Thank you," he whispered against her hair.

She looked up at him and he saw in her eyes all that he had loved and all that he had missed. The kiss he gave her was hot with the promise of passion. If he could, he'd claim her here and now. He'd almost died but she'd saved his life. She was sensitive, outrageous and brave, and despite the clawing pain in his arm, he wanted her like he'd never wanted her before.

"Trent." Her eyes shimmered. "He might be dead."

"C'mon." He turned his mind to the immediate—keeping her safe. "We've been compromised."

Despite her tears, she didn't hesitate, didn't flinch, just followed, and more important, she didn't ask questions.

They were two blocks away when she stopped him.

"Trent, you're hurt. Let me take care of it," Tara said. "I've had some experience, two levels of first aid anyway." They stopped at a little *farmacia* on the same block as the hotel. He waited outside and she went in. She was out in less than five minutes with gauze, ointment and antiseptic.

Back in their room, she laid out her supplies. "Take off your shirt," she ordered. "You were lucky, Trent." She cleaned the area around his upper arm and applied ointment.

He tried not to flinch as the pain rocketed down his arm and through his shoulder.

"This is my fault," she said and there was a tremor in her voice.

"No, Tara."

"You could have been killed," she said in a shaky voice. "You're lucky it only grazed your arm." She wrapped the wound with gauze. "You should really see a doctor, make sure—"

"No!"

She stopped, the gauze in hand.

"I'm sorry. I mean, no, we have to get moving. I don't think it will be a problem, you did a fine job."

"I know," she said. "I know. We need to get out of

here. I don't know what I was thinking." She looked at him with concern and fear in her eyes. "What do we do next?"

He took the disposable phone out of his pocket. He'd kept it overnight and already that had proved to be a mistake. But as long as he had it, he might as well make the defining call.

"I was waiting for your call," Jackson said. "We had a break in the case. There's been a string of armed robberies since the incident in Pueblo. It's like they're on steroids. The last one was here in Denver. One of the thieves is dead, along with a teller. But the good news is that we've finally got solid evidence linking Lucas Cruz to the bank robberies. We've also confirmed that the cartel his brother, Yago, belongs to has been recently active in Jalisco State. Yago Cruz is not a man you want to meet in a dark alley. His cartel is responsible for numerous murders."

"This only gets worse," Trent said. For Jalisco State was the one they'd just fled.

"I'm only speculating. But my thinking is that not only did Cruz hire his brother to take the witness out, Yago asked for more money. To get it, Cruz had to plan more robberies. There's been one a day over the last week in the Denver area. Sorry I don't have better news but at least now you know what you're up against. No more guesswork. The good news is that you'll be out of there soon."

"Can't be soon enough," Trent said. "I was just shot."

Jackson muttered an expletive and added a darker

curse as if it was an afterthought. "Yago's cartel has found you, but how? You haven't touched base with Carlos since you left Guadalajara?"

"No. Only you and Enrique."

There was silence at the other end. "Crap. We can't take any chances. Enrique was the only one you spoke to other than me. That's too coincidental. I don't want to point fingers but how else were you found?"

"You're suggesting—"

Jackson cut him off. "You need to cash out now and hit the road. Forget Enrique's plan to fly from there. It may be compromised. We'll fly you out from there straight up to El Paso."

Trent waited. He knew Enrique was now a suspect and out of the loop. He knew, too, that Jackson was thinking on the fly as his position often forced him to do. "I don't like where this is going. Just to be safe, we move to plan B. I'll get the details together and be in touch. It'll be a bit of a hop-skip at that distance. The guy I have in mind flies a helicopter and he'll have to refuel to get you to the border. But he should be available immediately and time is critical. From El Paso, we'll get you to Denver. Can you hold your position?"

"I'm not sure for how long."

"Contact me in three hours. I'll have the details sewn up then. We'll have you out of there soon. In the meantime, take care of yourself and hang low. And check out of that damn hotel. Find something else, now, on the other side of town."

"Goes without saying," Trent said.

He disconnected and glanced at Tara. Her face was white. But her chin was set in a determined manner.

"New arrangements are being made to get us out," he said. He took her hand. "We're out of this hotel."

"Why?" she said with worry heavy in her voice.

"Considering what happened, the original plan is compromised. We can't trust that they don't know about the plan to meet a small plane and fly out. They know we're here and what part of the city we're in. We'll have new arrangements in three hours' time. That's not long," he assured her. "The shooter is gone. And whoever they are, they won't get it together that quickly." He didn't mention Enrique's name. But the sequence of events kept playing through his mind and reminding Trent of the possibility of his deception.

The three hours passed uneventfully. They spent time on the fringes of a crowded beach and sat at a popular restaurant. Both were places where other foreign tourists frequented. With his sleeve covering his bandaged upper arm and their souvenir T-shirts, they looked no different than any other young couple.

When he gave Jackson a call, he received the final instructions that would get them out of Mexico, hopefully without incident and without further delay. They were leaving today.

"We're almost home, babe, almost home."

"Babe?"

He bent down and kissed her. "Always," he murmured. His left arm held her close and he vowed to himself that it always would.

Chapter Twenty-Seven

The helicopter flew them to the border city of Ciudad Juárez. From there, Jackson had arranged an expedited border crossing that took them to El Paso, where a Cessna was waiting to take them to Houston. This time there were no glitches.

Two days later, they were in the safe house that Jackson had arranged. Tara had become Jessa Banyon, and Trent was playing her husband, Jeff. For the next four months, the world would know them as the Banyons.

Trent looked over at Tara with a smile. "What are you thinking?" he asked.

"That one day I'd like to go back to Mexico. Despite everything that happened and why I was there, it's still a place I'd love to explore."

"That surprises me. Considering everything."

"Of course, without some of the excitement we had this time," she said and leaned her head against his arm.

He smiled down at her. He'd done more this trip than keep her safe. He'd found the woman who'd once been the girl he loved. And he'd discovered that he didn't love her anywhere near the same way he'd loved the girl—he loved the woman more.

She looked up at him. "Did I ever tell you thank you?"

"Thank you?" He frowned. "What do you mean?"

"For risking your life to save mine."

"It's what I do."

"And that frightens me," she said. "I'd hate to worry about someone I love every day, every waking hour."

His heart tripped. *Someone I love.* What did she mean by that? He didn't know if he dared hope if…

"I love you, Trent," she said. "That terrified me at first but when I had that gun in my hand and realized that I could save you, I lost my fear of a lot of things. It's strange. My grandfather's collection frightened me. But defending you changed all that. Actually needing the weapon I held in my hands made me realize their place, that it's not all death and destruction. Protection. Like you do." She turned to look at him and smiled, putting a finger to his lips. "I know that was a lot. No need to respond. Not now, we've waited all these years."

"Tara, I don't know what to say." He knew what he wanted to say but he wasn't ready. This wasn't something he could knock off without a thought and yet he should.

She smiled. "I know that you're good at what you do. And I'm not so scared of letting myself go. I mean, with my feelings." She paused as if for effect. "Let's give us a go."

Damn, he thought. That was his line.

"Definitely," he said and it was lame but in the moment it was all he had.

She leaned over and kissed him. It was a kiss that was full of promise and hinted at more as their tongues met and mated.

There were still weeks until the trial. He could only guess that the spark that had begun in a wild chase through Mexico would continue to grow. He couldn't see it being any other way.

Four months later

"I CAN'T BELIEVE that it's over," Tara said as she took Trent's hands in hers. "Can you?"

The crazy race to save her life was over and yet their life together was just beginning. The danger that they'd faced on foreign soil was gone. The danger they'd faced here at home was now behind bars. Jackson had been busy in the first weeks of their arrival home. There had been arrests. Lucas Cruz and two members of his gang were behind bars. A third was dead, killed by local sheriffs, after they'd pulled off two more bank robberies. Another was missing.

Unfortunately for Lucas Cruz, the two surviving members of his gang testified against him to receive less jail time.

In Mexico, Yago Cruz had been arrested by authorities and immediately gave up Enrique's name.

But it was easy to accuse a dead man. What was clear was that both the truck that tried to take them off the road outside Lake Chapala and the man who tried to shoot them in San Patricio had ties to the cartel. Unfortunately, only the shooter in San Patricio had been caught.

Only a week ago, Trent and Tara had moved back to her place in Pueblo. She'd wanted to get back to Pueblo, her house and her job. For him, it had been a no-brainer. Anything she loved, he loved, too.

"Armed robbery and murder. Lucas Cruz and his gang won't see the light of day," he said. "Hard to believe that the trial is done."

"And Carlos is free and clear. Thank goodness," Tara said as she pulled a knotted rope for a little brown, white and black puppy to tug. The puppy looked amazingly like Maxx, Carlos's dog. A second one with identical markings slept in her lap.

It had been a tough go for Carlos. A hard pill for the former cop to swallow. He'd been snowed and used by Enrique. The information he'd received from Enrique and relayed to Trent and Tara had taken them down that fateful road where Enrique had arranged to have them taken out by the man in the pickup truck. When that had failed, he'd tried again at San Patricio.

Enrique had paid for his crime. Although it hadn't been proved, the general consensus was that the cartel had taken him out before an arrest could be made. The one good that had come out of it was that the cartel was no longer a presence in San Miguel de Allende.

Despite the fact that Enrique had paid with his life, Carlos claimed that didn't clear him personally. He wanted to make it up to them, especially Tara. Besides offering free rent anytime they were in town, combined with an open invitation to visit, he'd offered something special to Tara. When a street dog gave birth to a tiny litter of two sired by Maxx beneath his patio, he'd been ready to give her one of the pups, knowing her love of dogs.

She'd told him that she wouldn't take one of the puppies unless Trent was on board with the idea. Trent had immediately vetoed it while secretly agreeing with her. A dog would be good for her after everything that had happened. He'd hated seeing the disappointment in her eyes when he'd lied to her. But it wasn't for long.

He'd contacted Carlos and arranged for the necessary shots and transportation for both pups. He had a plan that began the minute the puppies arrived and had time to recuperate from their flight.

"I still can't believe that you did this," Tara said as she held one of the pups in her lap. The other curled on top of her feet. "Or that you got both of them."

"Carlos snowed me a bit," he said with a laugh. "Said the little mites faced a harsh life on the streets. By the time he was done painting the picture, I was hooked. Besides, neither of these two will grow to any size and two small dogs can't be any more work than one."

She shook her head. "You're crazy but what a great gift."

"After everything that happened, I thought they'd give you some protection."

"Protection?" she laughed.

"Okay, consider them an alarm system. Not that you'll need it," he said. "You have me. And I won't let anything happen to you, babe."

"I know," she said. "I can't believe it. After all these years, we found each other. And we'll be married." She touched his hand as if reminding herself that this was all real. "It's a dream come true." She snuggled closer to him. "And these two. Puppies and a proposal."

"Don't forget the flowers," he said.

"Took a back seat." She laughed.

His laugh soon joined hers. They'd gotten engaged a week ago on a hot summer night under a full moon. Trent had outdone himself in the romance department, or so Tara had claimed after she'd said yes. He'd gifted her with the two pups in a basket, jokingly calling them their starter family. She'd said it was over-the-top romantic.

"I can't believe this is over," she said with a pensive look. "That the creep is in jail along with his thieving buddies." She smiled as the second puppy tried to scramble into her lap. She reached for the dog, and the ring that he'd given her glimmered on her left hand.

He bent to kiss her. The kiss morphed quickly

from gentle and soft to something hot and passionate. It was always that way with them, no middle ground.

"Let's take this show to another room," he said, his voice thick with desire. He glanced to his left, where paintings for her first exhibit were lined up, waiting for next week's show. The sight reminded him of her talent and her determination.

"Let's," she replied. She set the puppies down, took his hand and led the way.

The moonlight shone through the window and sparkled on the ring that he had given her, as if reflecting on the promises he'd made.

He'd made promises he knew he would keep. The easiest had been to love her forever. He knew that it would be as he'd promised; a life of dreams come true and a future that they would create together.

* * * * *

*Look for the previous book in Ryshia Kennie's
American Armor miniseries,*
Wanted by the Marshal,
available now from Harlequin Intrigue!

INTRIGUE

Available October 22, 2019

#1887 ENEMY INFILTRATION
Red, White and Built: Delta Force Deliverance • by Carol Ericson
Horse trainer Lana Moreno refuses to believe her brother died during an attack on the embassy outpost he was guarding. Her last hope to uncover the truth is Delta Force soldier Logan Hess, who has his own suspicions about the attack. Can they survive long enough to discover what happened?

#1888 RANSOM AT CHRISTMAS
Rushing Creek Crime Spree • by Barb Han
Kelly Morgan has been drugged, and the only thing she can remember is that she's in danger. When rancher Will Kent finds her on his ranch, he immediately takes her to safety, putting himself in the sights of a murderer in the process.

#1889 SNOWBLIND JUSTICE
Eagle Mountain Murder Mystery: Winter Storm Wedding
by Cindi Myers
Brodie Langtry, an investigator with the Colorado Bureau of Investigation, is in town to help with the hunt for the Ice Cold Killer. He's shocked when he discovers that Emily Walker, whom he hasn't seen in years, is the murderer's next target.

#1890 WARNING SHOT
Protectors at Heart • by Jenna Kernan
Sheriff Axel Trace is not sure Homeland Security agent Rylee Hockings's presence will help him keep the peace in his county. But when evidence indicates that a local terrorist group plans to transport a virus over the US-Canadian border, the two must set aside their differences to save their country.

#1891 RULES IN DECEIT
Blackhawk Security • by Nichole Severn
Network analyst Elizabeth Dawson thought she'd moved on from the betrayal that destroyed her career—that is, until Braxton Levitt shows up one day claiming there's a target on her back only he can protect her against.

#1892 WITNESS IN THE WOODS
by Michele Hauf
Conservation officer Joe Cash protects all kinds of endangered creatures, but the stakes have never been higher. Now small-animal vet Skylar Davis is seeking Joe's protection after being targeted by the very poachers he's investigating.

Get 4 FREE REWARDS!

We'll send you 2 FREE Books plus 2 FREE Mystery Gifts.

Harlequin Intrigue® books feature heroes and heroines that confront and survive danger while finding themselves irresistibly drawn to one another.

FREE Value Over $20

"Let's try this again." Logan wiped his dusty palm against his shirt and held out his hand. "I'm Captain Logan Hess with US Delta Force."

Her mouth formed an O but at least she took his hand this time in a firm grip, her skin rough against his. "I'm Lana Moreno, but you probably already know that, don't you?"

"I sure do." He jerked his thumb over his shoulder. "I saw your little impromptu news conference about an hour ago."

"But you knew who I was before that. You didn't track me down to compare cowboy boots." She jabbed him in the chest with her finger. "Did you know Gilbert?"

"Unfortunately, no." Lana didn't need to know just how unfortunate that really was. "Let's get out of the dirt and grab some lunch."

She tilted her head and a swathe of dark hair fell over her shoulder, covering one eye. The other eye scorched his face. "Why should I have lunch with you? What do you want from me? When I heard you were Delta Force, I thought you might have known Gilbert, might've known what happened at that outpost."

"I didn't, but I know of Gilbert and the rest of them, even the assistant ambassador who was at the outpost. I can guarantee I know a lot more about the entire situation than you do from reading that redacted report they grudgingly shared with you."

"You are up-to-date. What are we waiting for?" Her feet scrambled beneath her as she slid up the wall. "If you have any information about the attack in Nigeria, I want to hear it."

"I thought you might." He rose from the ground, towering over her petite frame. He pulled a handkerchief from the inside pocket of his leather jacket and waved it at her. "Take this."

"Thank you." She blew her nose and mopped her face, running a corner of the cloth beneath each eye to clean up her makeup. "I suppose you don't want it back."

"You can wash it for me and return it the next time we meet."

That statement earned him a hard glance from those dark eyes, still sparkling with unshed tears, but he had every intention of seeing Lana Moreno again and again—however many times it took to pick her brain about why she believed there was more to the story than a bunch of Nigerian criminals deciding to attack an embassy outpost. It was a ridiculous cover story if he ever heard one.

About as ridiculous as the story of Major Rex Denver working with terrorists.

Her quest had to be motivated by more than grief over a brother. People didn't stage stunts like she just did in front of a congressman's office based on nothing.

Don't miss
Enemy Infiltration *by Carol Ericson,*
available November 2019 wherever
Harlequin® Intrigue *books and ebooks are sold.*

www.Harlequin.com

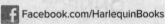

Love Harlequin romance?

DISCOVER.

Be the first to find out about promotions, news and exclusive content!

 Facebook.com/HarlequinBooks

 Twitter.com/HarlequinBooks

 Instagram.com/HarlequinBooks

 Pinterest.com/HarlequinBooks

ReaderService.com

EXPLORE.

Sign up for the Harlequin e-newsletter and download a free book from any series at **TryHarlequin.com.**

CONNECT.

Join our Harlequin community to share your thoughts and connect with other romance readers!
Facebook.com/groups/HarlequinConnection

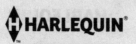

HARLEQUIN®

**ROMANCE WHEN
YOU NEED IT**

HSOCIAL2018